Looking for Derek

by N.C. Nest

Copyright © 2020 N.C. Nest

All rights reserved. This book or any portion thereof may not be reproduced or used in any manner whatsoever without the express written permission of the publisher except for the use of brief quotations in a book review.

For permissions or to contact the author, e-mail ncnest1984@gmail.com.

Dedication

The love in this story is for Bri. Infinity times cubed. He is my one and only.

The fact that you are seeing this new edition is due to Tapas. Tapas is a publishing app that gave this story an audience—thousands of readers that supported me, rooted for these characters, and related to these characters.

I wouldn't be who I am today if not for Bri. This story wouldn't be what it is today without for Bri and the people at Tapas.

Chapter One

I pretended to fall asleep next to Derek on the bus so my hand could touch his thigh. My fingers, progressing slower than an iPhone update, grazed the side of his legs. My heart raced and I panicked that Derek could hear it. Silly, I know, but it was probably also silly how much I enjoyed touching his leg. The risk of getting caught enhanced my excitement. It was the first time I had ever touched a boy in a way that wasn't platonic. To be honest, it was the first time I had ever really liked a boy, and with Derek, the attraction was immediate. More than a precarious urge, there was something magnetic, something uncontrollable about my desire. It was like seeing an ice cream cone on the first day of summer and needing a taste no matter the cost. I couldn't hold back. I wanted to open my eyes, to see if he noticed, to see if he reacted. Or—please God, please—to see if he liked it.

I was sixteen-years-old and on a charter bus from a small town in central Indiana to Kings Island amusement park in Cincinnati, Ohio. It was summer and I had won a trip from a fundraising company. My high school and virtually every other high school in the state used a company called For Fun and Service Fundraising, which sold everything from cookies to candles. The company was popular in schools for the prizes it gave away, and last year, they promised everyone who sold at least fifty items an entry into their Kings Island Getaway, a free trip from Indianapolis to Cincinnati. Out of everyone who sold fifty items in their particular schools, one person would be randomly selected. All you had to do was get a ride to Indianapolis and you'd get a free bus ride, overnight hotel stay, and a full day at the amusement park. I had been the winner from my school and Derek was from his. We had been driving for about sixty minutes, had first met about seventy minutes ago, and I had been . . . I guess you'd say in love or at least obsessed for about sixty-nine minutes now.

Daring myself to open my eyes, I couldn't believe the audacity that pulsed through my veins. Maybe it was the fact that I was on a bus full of strangers, cocooned next to this boy, unaware and apathetic to all the bodies in other seats. But something made my arms shake with adrenaline when Derek reached out his hand and introduced himself to me. It was something I had never felt before.

"Hey," he said. "Can I sit next to you?" He had thick, dark hair, gelled and spiked. Not a strand of hair would move, like a teen pop star in some outlandishly perfect Instagram pic.

"Sure," I mumbled, caught off guard. I was expecting a fun, random weekend just before my junior year of high school began. I expected butterflies from roller coasters, nausea from too many corn dogs, vibrations in my ears from the cacophony of carnival noises . . . not the tightening in my stomach when I shook his hand.

"I'm Derek," he reached out. That's when my arms started to shake. What was this feeling? What was wrong with me? Electricity pulses in my veins.

"I'm Nick," I managed to say through a dry throat.

"Nice to meet ya. You like roller coasters?"

"Yeah. You?" My voice cracked, and I tried to swallow the lump in my throat.

"Hell yeah. They're the best. I can't wait. This place has the fastest wooden roller coaster in the world, did you know that?" He grinned, revealing a cute half-moon dimple over a perfect smile.

"Yeah," I said, although I had no idea. "It sounds like a beast."

"That's what they call it!" He laughed. I caught myself staring at his lips and all I could think about was how they might feel against mine.

God, what's happening to me?

"What's that you're reading?"

I looked down at a book I had brought with me for the ride, but in that moment, the title, the story, and the characters had all vacated my mind. Derek followed my gaze and shouted, "*Game of Thrones*! Oh man, you're on the last book, too. I won't tell you what happens. But I've read it. It's so good."

"Yeah?" *Game of Thrones.* Okay, that's what I was reading. That was my favorite and that was his, too? Is the universe messing with me today?

"Who is your favorite character?" he asked.

I couldn't remember any of their silly names. I looked down at my book scrambling for a detail that would trigger my foggy memory. What the hell was wrong with me?

"I love Daenerys," he told me, after waiting a moment. "I love how she starts so innocent and sweet, but she's tough, you know? And she becomes a real bad ass, a fighter for those who can't fight for themselves. She's Martin's best developed character."

He paused and looked at me. Beautiful and smart? I couldn't think of a single guy in my school who actually talked about book characters like that.

"Have you seen the series?" he asked. I wiped my chin, afraid I was drooling.

"Uh-uh." And here I am, unable to say a complete word.

"Probably for the best. I won't spoil anything then," he said. "Except to say that I think they botched the ending. Books are always better."

He continued to comment while keeping it ambiguous so not to spoil anything. After a bit, he took out his phone and started texting someone. I cursed myself because I worried I was losing his attention and interest. My arms felt like they were floating, and my head was fuzzy. I've never felt an instant attraction before, and apparently, it came with a side-effect of mental paralysis.

I looked out the window in silence, trying to gather a coherent thought that I could articulate. I glanced over at him frequently, smiling at his smile.

I could feel the vibrations of the bus, a buzzing through my legs and back. I could smell the bus bathroom, an intoxicating, superfluous amount of disinfectant. Everything surrounding me stimulated my senses, as if I were hyper alert to everything, but I still couldn't think of a darn thing to say.

We had been silent for several minutes, too many minutes, and that's when I decided I was going to "fall asleep." If I couldn't use words, I'd show him how I feel somehow. But how?

I could touch him. Yes. I wanted to touch him. I needed to touch him. My hands had been clasped, as if I were afraid they'd shoot out to him, enticed by this magnetic attraction. The potent force of fascination demanded a response, and since my mouth couldn't act, I let my hands do the talking for me.

Okay, I know what you're thinking. Why don't I just ask him if he has a girlfriend and see how he answers? But you see, I wasn't thinking. And if you want to know the truth, the real kicker here: I had a girlfriend. We had been getting pretty serious, but I hadn't thought about her since the moment Derek shook my hand. I couldn't even think of her name in this moment. I closed my eyes, edged a bit closer to him so our shoulders were touching. I didn't feel him move or anything, so after a carefully timed minute, I let my hand fall off my knee. One hand just so happened to have enough momentum to swing gently towards his leg. It floated, glided, and rested right above his knee, inching towards his inner thigh.

It was as if he were pure electricity, and my hand was the cord. I felt charged, alive, my heart beating faster and feeling fuller than ever before, like filling up a tank with gas but letting it spill and soak the outside of the vehicle far after the tank was full. I decided it was time to open my eyes.

When I looked at him, he was still playing on his phone, but he must have sensed something because his head shifted, turned toward me, and then he smiled.

He smiled at me, and I about died.

"So you wanna be my partner?" he asked.

"What?" I gasped. My stomach dropped.

"On the roller coasters. Wanna ride them with me?"

"Yeah, for sure. That would be great." My hand was still there. He didn't seem to care. Or maybe he didn't realize it. Could that be possible? Before I could do anything else, a kid in the back of the bus stood and shouted a question.

"Anyone wanna play Bullshit?"

Shut up, I wanted to tell him, but I took my hand away from Derek's leg as the boy approached.

"Sure," Derek replied. He turned and looked at me. "You know it? It's a card game. You have to lie about what cards you're playing." I swear he looked down at my hand and grinned.

"Okay," I answered.

"It will be fun. After a few rounds, we should be there. And then it's time for roller coasters."

*****

We played cards for the next couple of hours with a group of guys and a couple girls. We laughed and the adult chaperones shushed us a few times if we yelled "bullshit" too loud. But all I wanted was to be alone with Derek.

We arrived at Kings Island, and I hoped we'd be alone then, but no, the entire Bullshit playing group decided to stick together.

We got to the first roller coaster, and Brandon, the guy who suggested the game in the first place, stood next to Derek in line.

"Dude, this is gonna be boss," he told Derek. I was getting pissed now. I was supposed to be Derek's partner. Why didn't he come stand next to me in line? On the first ride, Derek and Brandon rode as partners, and I rode with a girl named Jackie.

"What a rush!" she shrieked after the first ride. My gaze was in the distance. Derek and Brandon had already exited and were walking to the next ride. In a matter of hours, I had felt two of the most extreme emotions I had ever experienced. This second one was not enjoyable. There was a pressure behind my eyes and a boulder in my stomach. If I had possessed Jedi mind powers, the rest of this group would have been incapacitated a long time ago in my jealous rage.

Jackie and I caught up to Derek and Brandon at the next ride. "Hey," Derek said to all three of us. "Should we switch up partners?"

"Sure, if you want," Brandon said, disinterested, staring at the roller coaster.

"I'll ride with you," Jackie said to Derek.

Shit, I almost said out loud. But Derek looked at me, smiled knowingly, and said, "Alright, cool. And then I'll ride with Nick on the next one."

This ride could not get over soon enough. We waited in line for nearly thirty minutes, and it felt like a year had passed. No one talked. It was hot, we were soaking in our own sweat, and we were reminded of what amusement parks are really like during the summer: a bunch of people baking and sweltering under the sun waiting in line for hours to enjoy a sixty second thrill.

But the ride did come and go, and in line for the next one, Derek said, "I'll ride with you this time, cool?"

"Cool." I tried to keep my voice calm. Of course, this ride went much more quickly. I don't think we waited more than a few minutes, and then there we were: seated, a tired employee double checking our safety belts, my forehead burning in the sun, and a fresh breeze blowing in our faces as the ride began. And then the next amazing thing of the day happened. The ride jerked hard as it climbed a long hill, and when it jerked, Derek jumped and grabbed my knee with his hand.

And he left it there.

We climbed and climbed an enormous ascension, and I never wanted it to stop. We reached the top and the ride curved before its sharp, steep descent down. I turned and beamed at Derek, and he smiled back. The ride dropped and we screamed. He squeezed my leg, and in a pure, impulsive moment of bravery, I grabbed the hand that rested on my knee. Seconds later, the ride was over. I squeezed his hand gently, not wanting to take it away. He turned his head, his lips curled up, and his eyes sparkled. He squeezed my hand back, and my heart slammed against my chest.

I could have cried. I don't think I had ever felt such a wonderful emotion before.

People started getting off the ride. Slowly and regretfully, I pulled my hand away, but I didn't want to get up. Jackie and Brandon were seated behind us. They stood, and as I turned to get out, I saw Brandon's gaze was locked on us. He saw Derek's hand on my leg. I couldn't interpret his facial expression, but he wasn't smiling. I felt sick to my stomach.

In the matter of seconds, fear replaced my love buzz. Why should I care what anyone else thinks? I shouted the question at my brain, but my legs and arms still shook as I got out of the ride.

"I think we'll let you guys have some time to yourself," Brandon told us. Again, I couldn't read his tone. Was he supportive or disapproving? And why did it matter what this stranger thought anyway?

"Whatever, man," Derek said with such cool confidence. I looked at his broad shoulders and thick chest. Yeah, *whatever*, I wanted to say, too. Brandon was short and overweight. Derek looked like he hit the bench press every day. I was pretty thin and had never been in a fight, but one look at Derek and I felt pretty comfortable that we'd be okay if we were in trouble.

Brandon and Jackie left, and Derek looked at me, smiled, and asked, "So what next?"

"We have to try that fastest wooden roller coaster!"

"Absolutely. Let's do it."

We rode coaster after coaster that day. Some rides we just hollered and giggled. On one or two, I'd reach out to him. On one or two, he'd reach out to me. We didn't talk about it. We didn't try to explain it. I didn't even know his last name or what school he went to or where he lived. I was living in the moment and felt absolutely perfect.

And no steep drop on a ride could compare to the wonderful feeling I had inside when Derek held my hand. It was pure magic.

When the sun went down, we took a break to play some carnival games. The smell of fried food and sounds of bells called to us. "Should we play something?"

"Yeah. And then I think we need a funnel cake," I told him.

He looked around at the variety of games and chose basketball. All he had to do was make one basket, and he'd win any choice of stuffed animals.

"You know the rims are smaller here?" I asked.

"I'll take my chances," he said, holding on to the ball. Bending his knees into a slight squat, he threw the ball high in a beautiful arch.

"Yeah!" I cheered as the ball swished through the net.

"I'll take that one," he told the attendant, pointing at a stuffed lion. He then handed it over to me and said, "For you."

"Thanks." All the dentists and all their drills in the world couldn't remove the smile from my face.

I wanted to tell him how much I liked him. I know it had only been hours, but I had never felt like this around another human being before. He made me feel . . . fully alive.

"You're really cool, Derek." I kicked at the concrete under my feet. *Stupid, Nick. Stupid.* You can do better than that.

But Derek reached out to me and grabbed my hand, not even once glancing over his shoulder to see who was watching. My stomach dropped and tingles erupted in every inch of my arms at his touch. "You're really cool, too," he told me and smiled.

He let go of my hand and gently punched me in the shoulder. I wanted to hug him. I wanted to kiss him. But I didn't know how to act. We were surrounded by who knows how many people. Derek didn't seem to care, but I didn't know what to do.

We played a couple more games, and then sadly it was time to go. The fundraising company paid for a hotel stay for the group so we didn't have to drive home late at night. Unfortunately, the adult chaperones had already arranged who was staying with whom. We each were stuck in a room with four people, and Derek and I were not assigned the same one.

After we checked in, I showered and got ready for bed. My brain was buzzing, and I could even still smell the funnel cakes and elephant ears. Like salt from an ocean swim, it lingered in my senses. I was rooming with Brandon and two other guys from the trip I didn't know, and I was eager to get to bed so I could see Derek again in the morning. It may be hard to sleep, but all I wanted in that moment was to fast forward time until I got to sit next to him for the long ride home. But right when I went to bed, there was a knock on the door.

Brandon opened it. Derek stood outside in the hall. "Hey," he said. "Can I stay with you guys?"

"This room is already full," one of the other boys yelled.

I sat up. *Of course he could stay!* But before I found the will to speak up, Brandon told Derek, "Go back to your own room, faggot." And he slammed the door shut. He looked at me, as if testing me. I was frightened. I was mad. I didn't know what to say or do. It was late at night. Suddenly, I was shaking. My mouth and body felt paralyzed. My lips parted, but I couldn't find any words to speak. Brandon stared at me, like a wolf trying to control a pack. A million thoughts swirled in my mind. I should leave the room and go to Derek if nothing else, but Brandon turned the lights off and I sat up in bed staring at the wall.

I could just talk to Derek in the morning, right? It was late after all. He'd understand, right? I rolled over and tried to fall asleep, dreaming of the ups and downs of the day, like riding the coasters all over again. But this time fear kept me from doing what I most wanted to do.

*****

The next morning we loaded the bus to get home. Derek sat in the back next to someone else. "Hey," I greeted, confused. "Wanna sit up here with me?" I asked ever so quietly.

"Nope. I'm good." He pulled out his phone and ignored me. My heart snapped. Like literally—I felt such sudden, quick pain in my chest and a terrible force in my head behind my eyes.

"Derek, I'm sorry," I said.

"GO AWAY." He didn't take his eyes off his phone.

I sat by myself on the ride home. Brandon, Jackie and some others played cards, but they didn't invite me or Derek to join. I stared at the same page of my *Game of Thrones* book the entire ride home. I kept thinking of things I could say or do. I kept asking myself why I was such a coward. Why didn't I leave the room and go after Derek? Why didn't I say something when Brandon called him a faggot?

My phone went off and I had a text from Darcie, my girlfriend. 'How was the trip?'

I thought of replying: *well, I met this guy and kinda fell in love I think. Surprise. I had the best day of my entire life with him yesterday. And then I blew it last night. Fuckin' blew it. He won't talk to me or look at me or anything.* Of course, what I really typed was 'fine. How are u?' And of course I didn't really care how Darcie was.

The bus had arrived in Indianapolis. It was time to go home. I exited first and thought of what I should say, what I could say to Derek to make up. It was my final chance to try something. I found a piece of paper in my bag. I wrote my full name on it, my cell phone, and my e-mail. Derek walked right past me in the parking lot.

"Derek," I called. He turned around. His eyes: I swear to you I had never seen such sadness in someone's eyes before. It was clear to me then that I had really hurt him, that I had completely messed up. "I don't even know your last name. Or where you go to school."

"I know." He turned away from me.

"Wait," I said.

"What?" he snapped, and if it was possible, his eyes were even darker.

"I'm sorry. I don't know what to say. Here, take this."

"What is it?"

"My name and number. I'm really sorry. Will you at least call? Derek, I . . . uh, I . . ."

I love you. That's what I thought. I know it's stupid. I know it had only been one day. But it's what I thought in that moment.

He took the paper with my name and number, then crumpled it up, threw it on the ground, and turned around without giving me any response.

If it only takes a moment to fall in love or feel infinite happiness, let me tell you: it takes even less time to fall into bottomless depths of sadness. I watched him walk away, I looked down at the crumpled piece of paper I had tried to give him, and all I could think about was that he was gone. Completely gone and out of my life.

Forever.

Chapter Two

I had two weeks until school started again, marking the beginning of my junior year. I spent those two weeks locked in my room listening to every sad song I could find. I even searched the internet and YouTube for "saddest songs ever." From eighties ballads my parents loved to the newest Taylor Swift songs that I once argued made me puke all found their way onto my playlist.

I had never felt like this before. Seriously. And no, I'm not some Bella *Twilight* chick in a dude's body. I've never been one to lock himself in his room, to ignore the world, to hate the world. But then I guess there's a first time for everything.

My name is Nick Revel. You must be wondering about me. Who is my girlfriend? Am I some gay closet case? Have I always known I liked boys? Am I bisexual, pansexual, or even just sexual?

Honestly, I didn't even know what pansexual meant until I looked it up online, and no, that doesn't sound like me. Here's the situation. I've been dating Darcie McCoy since last April. She's the first girlfriend I've ever had. I like her, but it's not the same attraction I have with Derek. I didn't even know I could have that attraction with someone until I met Derek.

Darcie's cool, but she's not (a boy?) Derek.

I'm a virgin. Maybe my label should be hand-sexual because my own hand is all I've really ever known.

Confused? Yeah me, too.

Okay, I'm kind of lying. I'm not completely confused. I just don't know how to be me. Yeah, I've always been attracted to guys. On the basketball team last winter—oh yeah, I play basketball, and I'm pretty good— our former captain Adam started what he called a "sword fight" in the locker room. He got all the guys to compare dick sizes. They were shaking their penises at one another, and I wasn't at all confused then: I thoroughly enjoyed what I saw but I had to hide in a bathroom stall. My sword was standing straight, and that wasn't something I wanted them to see.

So, am I just another classic closeted high school gay boy? I don't know. I mean, I do like girls, I think. I like Darcie. She's fun. She's a great kisser and I do like her boobs. Until I met Derek though, I had never felt something so powerful, and whatever it was I felt towards him, I had never felt towards Darcie or anyone else.

Which brings me to my two weeks of sad music. I found this really cool song by Phil Collins called "I Wish It Would Rain." I've been listening to that every day, and not once has it actually rained. It's been hot, dry, and depressing. That's August for you. That's love and life as well, I guess.

"Lover" by Taylor Swift comes on next. "Could I go where you go," I find myself singing and thinking of Derek.

Where is he? I wouldn't even know where to start looking.

The sadness hasn't stopped me from jerking off though. I've been rubbing one off to pics of Vin Diesel every night. I guess that should tell us something. I listen to sad music and then rub one off: it's the only way I can get to sleep. Don't judge me. I'm sixteen. What sixteen year old doesn't jerk off like every day?

Now it's the Saturday night before school starts, and I've got a date with Darcie. We're going out to a movie again. That's all we ever do, and most of the time we don't even watch the movie. We get there early, sit in the back row farthest from the screen, and make out. I don't even know why we pay the money to see a movie when all we do is make out. It's been getting kind of boring as of late.

But now fast forward out of the two weeks of binge-listening to sad songs and here I am, out of my depressing room, sitting in a dark movie theater with my arm around Darcie's shoulders. The previews are finally over, which means she'll probably lean in to start sucking face anytime soon. Moments later, like clockwork, she kisses me and sticks her tongue down my throat. We've been playing a lot with our tongues, like a thumb war in our mouths. It's something to do. I put my hand up her shirt and feel her boobs. They feel like small water balloons, and I like how hard her nipples get and the tiny bumps around the nipple. We did this for a few minutes, and then she did something to me for the first time ever.

She put her hand in my pants. She felt my penis. She's never done this, and I panicked for a moment. She held it at first, and then squeezed a little. Then she slid her hand up and down. I moaned a bit out loud, my panic increased, and I tried to keep quiet. I considered telling her to stop, but then the pleasure jumbled my thoughts into an incoherent nothingness. Numb. That's how my brain felt. Thankfully, no one else sat up here by us. We typically picked movies that have been out for a few weeks so they aren't too crowded.

She stroked me faster and faster, and I took pride in how hard I felt. It's as hard as concrete, a tree trunk, pure steel. I got to that point where I'm about to shoot, and I didn't know if I should warn her.

Oops. Too late.

My pants felt wet, and she removed a hand that looked like it's been covered with glue. She gave me a look somewhere between hot and gross and whispered in my ear, "I'll be right back." I assumed she needed to wash her hands, and I hope she does, or I'm not sharing my popcorn with her.

When she returned, we watched the rest of the movie in silence, and later I dropped her off at her house and kissed her goodnight.

"Did you have fun tonight?" she asked me.

"Yeah," I said.

"Really? You barely said anything the rest of the night."

"We were in a movie," I defended.

"Yeah but on the way home. You didn't even suggest we get food or anything. You drove me right here." She frowned and stared at me with those sad, puppy dog eyes. Darcie was a very pretty girl. She had these cute freckles all over her face and shoulder-length auburn hair, more brown then red, I guess. She looked cute when she was sad, but that cuteness was beginning to wear off on me.

"Oh, I'm sorry. I don't know where my mind is. I think you distracted me," I tried to joke.

She laughed, and I smiled, thinking my lie of a joke worked. "Oh, okay. That's good." And she kissed me again. "Okay, text me when you get home."

"I will," I lied again. I've spent all night with you and you want me to text you in five minutes when I get home? Jesus.

"Good night."

"Night, Darcie." I hooked my iPod up to my car radio and listened to that Taylor Swift song again on the way home.

It's hard being a teenage boy. I'm always divided that life is too much about sex or not enough about sex. What she did to me tonight felt great, but it makes me feel sad, too. It's weird how you can be happy and sad at the same time, especially over something that's supposed to feel good.

When I got home, my mom was waiting up for me as usual.

"Hi, Mom."

"Hi, honey. How was your date with Darcie?"

"It was fine."

"Just fine?"

"Yeah."

"I made you a snack. Mac and cheese in case you were hungry." She went to the kitchen, took the food out of the fridge, and put it in the microwave to heat up.

"Thanks, Mom."

"I've been worried about you," she said handing me the heated up mac and cheese. "You're always so active. The last two weeks, you've been alone in your room a lot. Care to tell me what's up?"

"I'm okay."

"How about you and Darcie?"

"I don't know. I'm just kinda bored anymore."

"Hmm," she said and sat down at the kitchen table with me. "Well," she continued, "that can happen when you're dating. Especially when you're young. The best thing you can do is be honest with her, you know? If you really like her, suggest doing other things than going to a movie. But if you don't really like her and you're bored, then maybe you need to consider moving on. The longer you wait, the harder it is going to be for the both of you."

"I know," I said even though I didn't. I had never broken up with anyone before.

"Is there anything else?" Mom asked. I often wondered if she knew more about me than she was telling. I always cleared my internet history and used Google Chrome's incognito feature whenever I looked up Vin Diesel pics or porn, but maybe she knows more because she's my mom.

Tonight wasn't the night to talk about the anything else though. I wasn't ready. I didn't feel like I'd ever be ready.

"No." I stuffed my face with the rest of the mac and cheese, hugged her, and kissed her goodnight.

"Thanks, Mom. I love you."

"I love you, too, Nick." I felt her watch me as I walked upstairs to my bedroom. But she didn't follow me or call out. She was a pretty cool mom, and I sensed that she made a deliberate effort to make herself available while also giving me space.

I took off my clothes, changed my sticky underwear, and laid in bed. With my headphones on, I listened to my music and stared at the stuffed lion Derek had won for me at Kings Island. I thought of what Darcie did to me tonight, and then I started to cry. I couldn't help it. I felt ridiculous, like a coward, like a baby. When was the last time I had really cried like this? Maybe never. Maybe this is what love and heartache do to you. I rolled and cried into my pillow so no one else would hear me. The problem with happiness, I had begun to understand, is that sometimes you get a taste of what is possible but realize that having it forever is impossible. That's what made me sad. I got every tear out and then I made myself a promise. It's time to move on, to be honest, to start junior year as a new person, a stronger person. Yes, I could do that. I will do that.

I fell asleep listening to my music, dreaming of the person I wanted to be, dreaming of the person I wanted to be with. Learn from the past, I told myself, but don't linger on it. Learn from Derek. Sure, maybe I'll never see him again. But I can at least make sure what I did to Derek is something I never do to another person ever again.

That's what I intended to do. That's what I needed to do.

Chapter Three

I feel like I get great ideas in the middle of the night, but then I wake up and forget the things I wanted to change. I didn't want to wake up to the person I was yesterday, but the urge to change and be someone new was overwhelming. I spent all of Sunday afternoon before school searching for Derek online. I woke up thinking about Derek as often as I woke up with morning wood, which was pretty much every day. Maybe I'd move on eventually, but I had to try everything I could, right?

Going online, I searched for every combination I could like "Derek Kings Island" hoping he'd have posted something on the internet that would take me to him. I tried the fundraising company website to see if they listed winners. All their website said was "congrats to all of our winners- you will be contacted directly." I searched every "person you may know" on Facebook named Derek. I tried Twitter, Instagram, Snapchat, and everything I could possibly imagine.

And I came to this conclusion: I will never find him online. I don't have enough information, or maybe he's not online at all. I don't have a last name, a school, and town . . . nothing.

I stared at my computer screen for several minutes, thinking. And then I reminded myself of what I promised before bed last night: move on.

Hopefully my obsessions would last no longer than my morning wood.

I shut off my computer and went downstairs for breakfast.

My sister Jen was already eating. "Hey, save me some," I said, messing up her hair.

"I have to get here first to get any before your fat butt eats," she snapped back. Jen was about to enter the fifth grade at a new middle school. She had the same hair as me, only longer, a shiny brown that turned almost blond over the summer. At this time of year, we were both almost blond, but not quite.

"WHAT. EVER," I said. Whatever had become her new favorite word, as it does for most middle school kids, I suppose.

"Oh my gosh, what ARE you eating?"

As I tossed away the skin, I said, "We call this a banana in first world countries."

"You usually go right for the bacon. Mom cooked us each three strips."

"Maybe I'll have some later."

"Are you sick? What is wrong with you? You don't turn down bacon. Ever."

I laughed. "That grease is getting to your head. I'll be outside if Mom or Dad ask."

"And now you're going outside?"

"I'm going to read for a bit. I thought it'd be nice to be outside. That's all. Don't get all problem child on me."

"Whatever. More bacon for me."

Peace and quiet. That's all I wanted, as I sat down on a bench we had in the backyard. That's when my cell phone went off.

It was a text from Darcie. Of course it was.

Morning, sunshine. What are you doing today?

Not replying to you, I thought, and put the phone away. I sat and read for nearly an hour without distraction until my Dad decided to come out.

"Hi, Nick. I was thinking I'd trim all the bushes today. Feel like helping your old man?"

Dad was a pretty good guy. Naive, in a *Modern Family* Phil Dunphy kind of way. He worked hard supervising construction projects. He was thick like the bushes he wanted to trim, but mostly muscle with a little beer gut. Dad did like his beer.

"Not really. But I can. If you really *need* the help," I generously offered.

"Funny. Grab both trimmers from the garage. This bush is getting as hairy as you. Time for a trim."

"Dad! I'm not hairy. I have like two hairs on my chest."

"Man to man, Nick. You may want to consider trimming the downstairs, too. I know it's not your sister who's dropping pubes all over the toilet."

"Dad! That's gross!"

"Don't say I didn't tell you when YEARS DOWN THE ROAD your girlfriend complains."

"Can we just trim the bushes?"

"That's what I'm talking about!" He grinned.

"Something is seriously wrong with you." I got the two trimmers, and we teamed up on a series of bushes on the side of the backyard.

"Mom tells me that you and Darcie are having problems. Everything okay?"

I really didn't want to talk about it anymore, but there was something about working with your hands and being outdoors that made me feel more open.

"I'm just bored. I spent every weekend with her, and she texts and calls all the time. We're not married. A guy needs his space, don't you think?"

"Young love can be very passionate, Nick. If you felt as strongly about her as she obviously does about you, I don't think you'd mind all those calls and texts."

I shrugged. "So does that I mean I should break up with her?"

"Life is funny. There was one girl when I was in high school that I dated every year except for freshman year. We'd date for a few months, break up, get back together, and we repeated that cycle until we graduated."

"What happened in the end?"

"She went away to college, and I met your mother. I suppose, like you, I got bored with the first girl. But then I got bored without her. It was a no-win situation. Bored with, bored without."

"So you're saying I might end up back with her even after we break up?"

"What I'm saying is you have to find something that excites you. Friends, hobbies, or the one girl that's just right for you. Then, even when you're bored, you'll be happy. You know, I think kids worry too much about being bored. When you're bored, you have time to think. That's not bad. And if you're happy overall, those moments of boredom aren't bad. They're relaxing, in fact."

Dad looked over the bushes and at me. We hadn't talked like this in quite a while. I suspected Mom put him up to it, but I didn't care. Dad was genuine. He wasn't much of an advice-giver throughout my childhood, but when he did, it seemed real and from his heart.

"I've been bored a lot this summer."

"We've noticed. I'll tell you something else. You may want to give your old friends a call. Bros before . . . Well, you know, as they say. You guys seemed to drift apart this summer."

I had a few good friends, mainly from the basketball team. "Yeah, Darcie took all of my time."

"You gave her all of your time. You have to find balance."

"Open gym for basketball starts next week. I'll get back into the game, back in shape, and back with my friends."

"Good. Now, hand me that hose. This bush looks quite dirty."

Without thinking about it, I handed Dad the hose and turned on the water. It wasn't the bush that he found dirty, evidently.

"Dad!" I shouted as he soaked me. Mom and Jen ran outside. I grabbed Dad and wrestled him to the ground. Mom and Jen got the hose and soaked both of us.

"Ugh, what's wrong with you people?" I yelled.

I ran towards them, pulled the hose out of their hands and got them back. We were all so wet that we fell to the ground laughing.

It was moments exactly like this one, you see, that I was scared I would lose if I ever told my family the truth.

*****

I took Dad's advice and later that day got ahold of my friends.

I texted Asantà first. He was one of the forwards on the basketball team. I wasn't very tall, but I was quick and had a decent shot, so I played guard. Asantà was tall and fast, a very talented ball player. *Hey- been a long time, sorry. Ready for school tomorrow?*

UR ALIVE? We all wondered where u been.

I took a deep breath, thought of what to say, and sent him this reply. *With Darcie a lot. Sorry. I miss ball and you guys. We playin after school?*

YEP. Will be good to kick ur ass again. Ball is life.

I will bro.

I decided to text a few others from the team and call Darcie back. I didn't know what I wanted to do for sure, and with school just starting, it would be nice to have someone to go to all the football games with. So,I didn't mention anything about being bored or wanting more space (or, you know, preferring boys over girls).

"So you'll sit with me at lunch tomorrow?" Darcie asked as I was about to hang up and go to bed.

"Come find me and sit with the guys. I've barely seen them all summer."

"I thought we might have our own table," she whined. "Or you could sit with my friends."

"Tomorrow I want to sit with the guys. We have to talk about the upcoming season, okay? But maybe I can alternate days. One day with them. One day with you."

"Fine," she said in the way that was nothing but. I wasn't going to press the issue, though, and I pretended that I thought everything was fine.

"I should get to bed," I said.

"Okay." Long pause. Are we still doing the who-is going-to-hang-up-first game? Am I thirteen? Jesus.

"Okay then. Good night."

"Nick," she said followed by another long pause. I swear I was about to hang up when she said, "I love you." It was the first *I love you* in our relationship.

Well, fuck, I thought. I'm not *not* saying it. She'll be pissed and I don't want a fight on the first day of school. So I did the only reasonable thing I could. I told her, "I love you, too, Darcie. See you tomorrow." And I hung up quickly. We had plenty of nights where we'd say good-night over and over again to each other till the point I thought my brain was going to explode. I wasn't about to start that with "I love you." Not tonight.

Would you think I was a total loser if I slept with the stuffed lion Derek had won me? In case you might, I won't tell you that I did exactly that.

*****

My school was called Worthlapp High, about thirty minutes outside of Indianapolis. It had developed the more common name of

Worthless High by the student body. And of course in an attempt for fun alliteration, we were the Worthlapp Wasps. The cheerleaders would wear stingers on their butts during pep rallies. It was all rather absurd, which is synonymous with high school.

We had one openly gay kid at Worthless High. His name was Steve. He was a sophomore and I swear he must have come out of the womb flaming and waving a rainbow flag. He started a gay-straight student alliance that I never attended. As far as I know, only a few empathetic freshman girls attended his club. You might hate me for what I think, but I really didn't like Steve. I just wanted to fit in. I never had dreams of coming out or taking a boy to prom. Maybe I'm some kind of homophobic closeted gay kid. I mean, if I'm being honest, I'm scared to be like Steve. And doesn't homophobia start with fear of what we don't understand? I just didn't want to be in the spotlight, I guess. I wanted to be seen as a regular dude, not the gay kid in school.

And maybe that's the problem. Maybe we need people like Steve to fight until we're all seen as regular dudes, no matter our sexuality.

Ugh. It's all so overwhelming sometimes.

I used to think things weren't so bad for Steve or gay kids today. The history books tell us we had a President of the U.S. who for the first time came out in support of gay marriage. Obama sounded cool. According to our lessons, the Supreme Court made marriage equality law of the land not that many years ago. There was a gay character or two on almost every TV show now, too.

But then the pendulum swung. That's how my history teacher described it. Change didn't make everyone happy, and often the next person in charge would be someone whose cause was to strip away at equality and progress.

I don't know if the world is okay or not.

And it makes me even more scared to speak up, honestly.

You see, if there wasn't still some kind of problem, then I wouldn't have this attitude that I just wanted to fit in and not be seen as different. It shouldn't be seen as different, not really. Different as in there are guys and there are girls and they are certainly different, but not different like there's good and bad. And to some, especially in a smaller school like mine, there is different good and there is different bad.

I didn't want to have to make a difference just by being who I was. I wanted to be happy and fit in. And if you can't tell, my mind loops around in this poor circular reasoning over and over again.

My skin crawled when people made jokes about Steve, though. Maybe the vast majority of people didn't hate or discriminate, but they still made fun of differences.

"There's Princess and his paparazzi," Asantà joked after school as Steve and the girls who attended his club meetings walked by. The rest of the team laughed, and I forced a smile.

Part of me wanted to speak up and say something to Asantà, to say that it wasn't cool to talk or think like that. But he wasn't hating on Steve, not really. He was trying to be funny. And if you haven't figured it out yet, I also didn't want to be the one who had to stand up and speak out. I hoped someone else on the team would do that.

"He walks like he has a thong lodged up his ass," Jared, our tall basketball center, added.

"I'm sure there's more than a thong up there." Zack laughed. Zack was our other guard, short and quick like me.

"You say that like you've been there, Zack. You and that big black dick." Toby snorted. Toby was our other forward along with Asantà. Zack, Jared, and Toby were seniors, while Asantà and I were juniors, but we got pulled up to varsity last year. The five of us were the Worthless High Wasps proud starting line-up.

"You just be jealous of what I'm packing," Zack told Toby, grabbing his own package for emphasis. I had to look away.

"We playing today or talking about your dicks?" I tried to change the subject.

"Didn't mean to leave you out, suga," Zack said and grabbed my balls. "You got a nice package yourself. For a white boy." The rest of the team laughed, and I smacked Zack's hand. I often wondered why straight guys liked talking or thinking about dick as much as I did. And these guys could get pretty friendly, like their legendary locker room sword fights. It was messed up.

"Let's play some ball, yo," I joked back, desperate to stop thinking and start playing.

*****

Guess who was waiting for me after practice? Yes, of course it was Darcie. She sat in the bleachers by herself watching us for about the last half hour. It was the five of us starters and a few other guys, nothing formal, only open gym this time of year. Basketball season wouldn't start for several weeks. First we had to get through the school's proudest sport: football. I wanted to support all the sports and not be a douche, but the football guys made it very hard. They were confident that their sport was the only one that mattered, and they were always happy to point out that they had bigger crowds.

"Hey, you wanna play some *Call of Duty* later?" Asantà asked me. I looked over at Darcie who waved too enthusiastically. Asantà saw her too and followed up, "Oh. Never mind. I see the ball and chain is here."

"No, man, I'll play. Let me say hey to her and I'll be over in a few."

"Cool." Asantà held out his fist and I bumped it with mine. "The rest of the guys will be there, too."

I jogged over to Darcie who wrapped her arms around my sweaty shoulders and kissed me long and hard, tongue and all. She held on for about ten seconds before I broke free and caught my breath.

"Well, hello to you, too." I laughed.

"I just missed you." She frowned.

"And I missed you," I lied, putting my hand under her chin and pulling her head up.

"Really?" She smiled and her eyes grew. This was another game I always had to play. She needed me to say every compliment at least twice.

"Yes, I really missed you," I repeated and pulled her auburn hair back over her ears. I kissed her on my favorite, or what used to be anyway, freckle on her cheek.

"We haven't talked since last night. You hung up so quickly."

"Oh, sorry. I knew it was going to be our first day back and with practice and all I wanted to be fully rested."

She frowned again, clearly dissatisfied. She remained silent. I think she was hoping I would be the first to say those other three words again. But I held my ground and stared back at her. She lasted about six seconds.

"I love you," she said.

I blinked, swallowed, put on my poker face and said, "I love you, too."

"Really? You mean it?" Here we go again repeating ourselves.

"Yes, I love you," I lied. God, am I a terrible person?

"And I love you," she replied. "Yay! My parents are cooking a big meal in honor of the first day back at school. You should come. They'd love to have you over."

"I promised Asantà I'd hang with him and the guys."

Her lower lip completely sucked in her upper lip. The classic Darcie disappointed frown. "First, you have lunch with them. Then you play after school. And you're gonna hang with them tonight? Where do I fit in this picture?"

"Darcie, I haven't seen them like all summer. It's important for a team to bond. I can't ditch them whenever my girlfriend wants to hang."

Her upper lip went entirely missing then. I regretted what I did next, but I couldn't help it. I laughed. Out loud. At Darcie's disappointment.

"What is so funny?" she snapped.

"Sorry." I laughed louder. "It's just . . ." more laughter. "When you're mad . . . you look like you only have one lip."

She gasped and her eyes went wider than I've ever seen them and that made me laugh even louder.

"I'm sorry," I tried. "What I meant was…" *Poker face, Nick, poker face.* "You look so freakin' cute when you're mad. It's adorable. I can't help but smile."

That did the trick. Her face softened, her upper lip slowly escaping the trenches of disappointment. "So, you still gonna ditch me tonight?"

"I'm not ditching you. I had plans with the guys first. I promise I'll sit with you at lunch tomorrow, okay?"

"Ohh kay." She pouted. "I love you."

Sigh. "I love you, too. See ya tomorrow." I gave her a quick peck on the lips, far less passionate than the soul sucking kiss she gave me earlier, then turned and sprinted out of the gym. Somewhere behind me I heard, "Call me when you get home tonight."

I'll pretend I didn't hear that, I thought.

Chapter Four

Friday was the first football game of the season for the Worthless High Wasps. I managed to talk Darcie into going with me and the guys. She wanted to go just us two, which was code for she wanted to hang under the bleachers and make out. I was tired of Darcie's tongue in my mouth, if you couldn't tell, so I told her we should hang with the guys. I had been rebuilding my friendship with them over the last couple of week since school had restarted. I enjoyed the guys, even if they were a bit crude at times, but hey, look who's talking here.

"You know what pisses me off though," Asantà started as we climbed the bleachers for a seat. "We come and support the football team every week. Rain, snow, it don't matter. How many of them come to our games?"

"Not enough," Jared added, taking a seat in the midsection of the bleachers.

"Hey," some mom called from behind Jared. "Can you boys please sit higher up? You're so tall, I can't see."

Jared laughed and looked at Asantà, who even as a junior was the unofficial leader of the group. "Sure, ma'am, we'll move up a few rows," Asantà agreed.

"I'd rather sit at the top anyway," Zack said.

"Yeah, we can spit on people walkin' under the bleachers." Toby grinned.

"You guys are disgusting." Darcie shook her head, holding my hand. "No wonder you don't have girlfriends."

"I date after basketball season. Dump 'em right before. That keeps my head in the game," Asantà told her and then gave me a disapproving look. For as close as I had been getting to the guys, it felt like they weren't all that enthused about Darcie.

I didn't say anything and made the mistake of smiling. Darcie took her hand away and crossed her arms. But that didn't stop her from following us to the top of the bleachers.

"Look at all the cheerleaders." Toby sighed. "They have a squad twice the size of ours. Stupid football."

"You know who else has something twice the size of yours?" Zack laughed and grabbed his crotch.

"Your mother?" Toby asked. "Yeah, she's a fat ass."

Zack hit him on the shoulder. "Don't you diss my ma."

"Don't diss my junk," Toby told him. "I'll pull it out right now."

"How can you take this?" Darcie asked me.

I laughed. "Welcome to my friends' world." She frowned and shook her head again and then looked down beneath the bleachers.

Asantà saw her staring. "Thinkin' of joinin' the herpes club? I wouldn't go down there and touch anything. Bunch a nastiness down there." She looked at him with a snarl on her face but didn't say anything.

The game was about to begin. The other team, who knows who they were or where they were from—we didn't pay attention to those details unless it was basketball—kicked off and the Wasps received. Our football team was supposed to be great this year. They made it to state nearly every year, although they hadn't won a state championship since before I was born. Always so close, but never good enough. The story of our lives, right?

Receiving the kickoff, one of our star players caught the ball and ran all the way to the end zone, scoring on the first play of the game. Everyone jumped up and cheered. Almost everyone. We slowly stood up and clapped to be polite, but Asantà and I rolled our eyes at one another and clapped as enthusiastically as you would at a golf match. It was jealousy, sure. We never had screaming crowds like this at our games, but dammit we worked just as hard.

By halftime, the Wasps had a 21-0 lead, and the stingers on the cheer squad had about fell off from all the ass-shaking. The best part of a high school football game finally arrived: halftime. This is when we'd walk around, talk, say hey to other classmates, grab some snacks, and most likely not care enough to watch the second half.

I ordered some nachos, to which Jared helped himself. "You could get your own, man."

"It's more fun to eat yours," he mumbled while crunching on a chip.

"Hey Asantà!" It was some of the JV basketball players gathered around the entrance of the stadium.

"What up?" He nodded. Never too social with the younger classes, Asantà was friendly but distant, the perfect way to be looked up to, he said. "If our program is ever going to be as popular as football, the kids have to want to be like us. So stay cool."

We walked around, the four guys, me, Darcie. She tried to reach out and hold my hand, and I ever so cleverly moved my nachos to the hand closest to her. Sorry, girl. This guy prefers processed cheese.

As I looked around at all the kids, parents, and teachers here at the game, I wondered: was life so boring that everyone has nothing to do but watch a bunch of teenagers run up and down a field? Yeah, it was that boring. And I felt even sadder for the older people here. Sure, you could say they were supportive. But supportive is another way of saying they have absolutely no life. And you know what Monday in every class would be like, right? All of the teachers who went would spend the first ten minutes of every class talking to the players about the game. Congratulating them, insulting the other team, applauding Coach God or whatever his name was, and making sure the kids knew how cool their teachers were to go and support the students' athletic efforts.

It was bullshit. It was like school existed to support the football team and that was all.

"What do you say we egg the football players' cars?" Zack suggested.

We laughed. "Hell yeah," Jared said. "Dude, your house is closest," he said to Toby. "Your mom got any eggs? Besides the dried up ones between her legs?"

"Fuck you. And yeah, we got eggs." Toby turned to Asantà. "What do you think?"

He looked at the crowd, ten times the size of the ones that supported our team. "Yeah, I'm in. Their cars will be easy to spot. The cheerleaders will have written on all the windows about how much they love them."

"Or how much they just want to suck their dicks," Jared said.

"Ain't that the truth?" Zack agreed. "They get blown for every point they score."

"I am having nothing to do with this," Darcie barked. "And you'll get in trouble, Nick. Don't you dare."

"You don't understand. Why don't you go home and I'll call you later?" I told her.

She huffed but replied, "You promise you'll call?"

I had to think about that. Would I really call her? Probably not. So instead I kissed her on the forehead and said, "I'll be careful. You shouldn't be here though in case we do get caught. Go. I'll talk to you later." I turned, threw one arm around Asantà and tried to throw one around Jared, but his waist was about my shoulder level. "Let's egg some football bastards," I said, and they all laughed.

We had to be quick. We knew that by the fourth quarter, people would start leaving. It would be best to egg sometime during the beginning of the third quarter. People would return to their seats, and the start of the second half would provide a temporary distraction.

Toby lived about two blocks from the high school. We jogged to his house and waited out back while he ran in the kitchen. He came out with one of the big boxes of two dozen eggs. Jackpot!

"Ma must have just went shopping. She'll be pissed as hell when they're missing, but I'll blame my little brother." Toby laughed.

He put them in a plastic grocery bag, and we ran back to the school. As we had hoped, no one was in the parking lot. The roars of the stadium let us know that the second half had started. Closest to the academic side of the school, two rows of cars had been decorated with "we love you" and "sting your way to victory." Yeah, these were those jackasses' cars. We each took a handful of eggs and aimed for the windshield of every one.

"Now this is a new kind of ball practice I could get used to." Zack grinned.

"Yeah, at least this way you score." Jared laughed.

"Whatev, freak," Zack joked back. We threw the eggs, splattering the cars, ruining some of the sweet letters of love the cheerleaders had written. We laughed so hard snot came out of Toby's nose and Jared snorted. It was awesome.

"We have to hide and wait for them to see," I suggested. "Their reactions will be even better."

"Yeah," Asantà agreed. "And this is perfect. They'll think the other team did it."

As bros do, we bumped fists and then went back into the stadium. We had way too much of an adrenaline rush to watch the game, so we continued walking around. As risky as it was, we even took a stroll down the visitors' section.

You see, even if we hated our own football team, there was some kind of school code where you had to hate the visiting team even more. It was the only way of having some kind of self-respect and redemption for our terrible behaviors.

"Boo!" the student section yelled when they saw us. We had the Wasp school colors on so we were easy to notice. *Black and blue, that's what you'll be too, when we're done with you,* the Wasp cheer team would chant.

"Wrong section, losers!"

"Don't say anything to them," Asantà cautioned us. "Here, we'll hang over there in the corner. Then we can wait till the game is over."

We nodded and followed him, and I scanned the crowd as we walked by.

And then my heart stopped.

And I stopped walking altogether.

My stomach hit the ground beneath my feet, and a wave of dizziness shot through me.

I spotted that black, perfectly gelled hair.

I saw those dark eyes—so passionate, mysterious, and beautiful.

He was watching the game, and he smiled, showing those picture-perfect teeth, that impeccable smile. The smile that had made me feel like the only person in the world.

Have I known you for twenty seconds or twenty years? Even song lyrics I once hated pulsed through my mind.

My throat dried up. *Could it really be him?*

"Nick, what the hell man? C'mon," I heard Asantà say. But I was frozen. What should I do? Should I go to him? Should I stand here until he sees me? But before I could decide, as if I ever would, Asantà and Jared grabbed me by the shoulder and dragged me along with them.

"What are you looking at?" Jared asked.

I shook my head and said, "Nothing. I thought I saw someone I knew. That's all. It's nothing."

Asantà looked at me closer. "Weird."

"Huh?" I asked.

"You look like you saw a celebrity or something. Like Lebron was here in the flesh," he said.

"Uh, yeah, I dunno." They pulled me away. I moved with great caution. This could be my chance. This could be my only chance! I stopped and turned again.

How many times will I let fear of what others think dictate my choices? I'm going to march right up to him. I'll say whatever it takes. He has to forgive me. He has to give me a second chance.

But now he was gone. *Had I imagined it?* He was there only seconds ago.

I scanned every row. I locked eye contact with every person in that section.

My mind must be playing tricks on me, or Derek is some kind of magician because once again, he had vanished.

Chapter Five

It was a little over a month into the school year, and it was homecoming weekend. Feeling like I had to, I had asked Darcie to the dance a couple of weeks ago. She had gotten a lot better at letting me hang out with the guys without too many problems. I still made the obligatory phone call each night before bed, and I had to have at least one night a week for the two of us to hang out alone. Don't get me wrong: it wasn't great, but I had gotten used to saying "I love you" and "I miss you" with a smile and without feeling too sick. Perhaps I should consider acting as a profession.

And what about Derek? You must be wondering if I went crazy since seeing him, or at least thinking I saw him, at that first football game.

Oh yeah, I went a little crazy. First, I figured out what team we had actually been playing. It was the Mayville High School Tornadoes. So I had another search term and tried every combination I could on Google and Facebook and everything I could think of once again. "Derek Mayville High" and "Derek Mayville Tornadoes." I searched through every online profile that listed "Mayville High" as the person's school, and I found a few Dereks, but not my Derek. I spent hours searching online and was absolutely no closer to finding him then I was the day after I got off that bus last summer.

I was frustrated, sure, but I had grown a thicker skin over the last month. And maybe some optimism. If I ran into him once, I'd run into him again. That's what I told myself, and I hoped to God that it would be true.

Now it was the Saturday of the homecoming dance. Mom and Dad had been cleaning the house. They insisted on me picking up Darcie, bringing her back, and letting them take some pictures. Dad was playing his old music quite loudly and singing to my mother while they cleaned. He was on a Meatloaf kick, some old rocker from the 70s who managed to have a couple of hits in the 90s too I think. The most popular song seemed to be "Paradise by the Dashboard Light." There was this great line at the end that made me laugh: "I swear I will love you until the end of time . . . and now I'm praying for the end of time to hurry up and arrive!" Dad sang this to my mom, jokingly, and she kicked at him. He picked her up and swung her around singing, "Cuz if I have to spend another minute with you, I don't think I could really survive!" My dad singing it made me laugh harder, and after hearing the lyrics, I thought that maybe I'll request the song at homecoming tonight to sing to Darcie.

Jen skipped into my room as I was getting dressed. "You look so handsome," she said.

I smiled at her and ruffled her hair. "Please don't ever grow up," I told her. "Please don't ever become a teenage girl."

"Okay," she said causally as if she could control it. "Can I help you with your tie?"

"You know how to tie a tie?"

"I asked Dad to show me so I could help you." She giggled.

"Okay. But try not to choke me."

"Oh, now you're giving me ideas!" She made me turn around so we both faced the mirror. "I can only do it if we're facing the same way." She draped the tie around my neck, looped the big part over the thin part, circled it around the top by my neck, and made the knot. Pulling the knot tight, she looked in the mirror and laughed.

"Oh, perfect. This is gorgeous!" I joked. "I think, though, that this is backwards. You know, this thin part is supposed to be behind the tie, not down past my waist."

"Let me try again!"

"Okay, you try again." She undid the tie and tried once more, this time getting it just about right. The back of the tie was still a little long, and the main part a little short, but I didn't care. She did a pretty darn good job for a ten-year-old.

"You look really great!" she complimented. She stood behind me on top of my bed while we looked in the mirror. "You have a little hair sticking up back here." She patted down the back of my head. I looked at myself in the mirror. I got a haircut, so it was shorter again, buzzed around the sides, very short brown on top. It had darkened a bit since I had been outside less, but was still a sandy kind of brown, the same color eyes to match. I felt too skinny though. Basketball practice every day had shed more weight, and I wished I had more muscle to go with it. These skinny arms. Maybe one day they'll be thicker.

I smiled and returned the compliment to Jen. "I'll never be as gorgeous as you." Jen's hair turned more of a brownish-red, not too different from Darcie's. Jen was a phenomenal sister. I had seen how some of my friends were with their siblings. I really did hope she never turned into a bitchy teenager. We kinda suck sometimes, but she still possessed an unadulterated optimism that I hoped never would change.

She gave me a hug, sat down on the bed, and said, "Do you wish you could go to homecoming with someone else?"

"What do you mean?"

"Mom and Dad say you don't really like Darcie."

"What else did they say?" I asked, sitting down next to her.

"I just overheard them talking that they were surprised you were still going out with her."

"That's all?"

She hesitated for a moment, tilted her head up, and said, "I think so. I was just curious. Is there anyone else you like?"

Oh, if only I could tell you. It would be the talk of the town.

"Maybe," I admitted. "But Darcie is my girlfriend. It's weird. I feel like I've been too busy to see her but too busy to break up with her. I'm just going with the flow, you know?"

"So who would you rather go out with?" Jen asked.

"Lots of questions!" I tried to smile. "What about you? Are there any boys you like?" Changing the subject to something about the other person was the best way to avoid talking about yourself.

"No. Boys smell. Lots of girls in my class already have crushes and boyfriends. Some have even kissed boys."

"That's pretty fast for fifth graders."

"That's what Mom says."

"Mom's right. I'm glad you're not rushing or trying to be like some of these other girls. Let things happen when they are supposed to happen."

"Yeah. I just want friends."

"That's the way to go."

"I'm not stupid, you know. I know that you changed the subject. So? Who do you like?"

"You are too smart for your own good."

"You're my big brother. I like knowing what you think."

I paused for a moment to look at her. She really was growing up too fast. Part of me craved to tell someone the truth, a yearning to get the weight off my chest. Once something is spoken aloud, you can't take it back, though. I was guarded and hesitant, and I wondered how she would react. Would she think it was gross? Would she have no judgment at all? Of course, if I confided in her, then she might tell our parents, and I wasn't ready for that yet.

"I don't know," was all I could say.

"I think you do."

"It's . . . complicated."

"What's his name?"

I almost fell off the bed.

"What did you say?" I asked her.

"What's his name?" she repeated. No emphasis on the "his." Strictly matter-of-fact.

I didn't know what to say. "What do you mean? I don't . . . "

"I don't care. I'm just guessing. There has to be a reason you don't want to say, so I'm guessing it's a boy."

"Oh my God, do you think Mom and Dad know?"

"I knew it!" She laughed.

"Don't laugh!" I felt my heart jump into my throat again.

"No, not about that. Boys, girls, nobody cares anymore. I just knew I was right!"

"Please don't tell Mom or Dad."

"I promise. But if you want me to be quiet, you have to do me one favor."

"And so the blackmail starts."

"You have to tell me who he is, silly," Jen said and poked her fingers in my ribs.

I smiled at her. *Thank God for little sisters.* "Okay, well, you remember the trip I went on last summer . . ."

*****

I was beyond ready for this dance to be over after an exhausting day. I came out to the first person ever and then I had to go pick up my girlfriend. Take pics with her family. Then take pics for my family. The irony gave me a headache, and I wasn't sure how much longer I could maintain this fake smile. We did dinner with the guys and their dates. They still didn't have girlfriends, but they each had asked someone to the homecoming dance.

Then the dance itself. Okay, let me explain two things. First, I can't dance. So all of the fast songs make me feel embarrassed.

Asantà, Zack, and Toby tore up that dance floor. They were awesome. Jared and I became wallflowers. Neither of us could keep a beat nor dance any kind of move. This of course pissed Darcie off. She wanted to dance, and when I said, "You know I can't dance," she'd put on that pouty face and try to dance with Asantà or Zack or Toby. Their dates gave her an evil look, but she held her ground, and every now and then, Asantà would turn and dance with her, perhaps out of pity.

Second, there were of course the ridiculous slow songs, and I was obligated to dance with her on those. The whole time I wanted to be home. I'd rather be talking with Jen. It felt so good to finally tell someone about what I really wanted, who I really was. It was euphoric. My defenses came down for the first time in my life and I was okay. More than okay. I was enchanted with the power of truth. I not only survived; I actually wanted to talk more about it. But here I was dancing with Darcie, keeping quiet. Two steps forward and one step back.

The dance finally ended in about ten years. Or a few hours. But you know, it felt the same. I drove Darcie to her house and was ready to kiss her goodnight and get back home.

But she had other plans. "Please come in," she said at her front door.

"I'm really tired, Darcie."

"You're always tired or busy. Tonight is our night. Please come in. Just for a little while."

"Okay." I gave in. My world didn't have to change in one night, I guess. I would try to be a nice guy.

We walked upstairs to her bedroom, and she turned on some music. "Where are your parents?" I asked.

"I thought you'd be happy to know that they won't be back for a couple of hours. They went to a party. They told me they'd be home around one. That gives us two hours alone."

Wonderful. *Oh shit, what did she think was going to happen tonight?*

She lit a couple of candles in her room and turned the music up. "Come here," she held out her arms. I walked towards her, and she wrapped her arms around me like we were slow dancing again. She kissed my neck, and the kissing morphed into sucking. I felt uncomfortable and loosened my tie a bit more. That was a bad move. She interpreted that in her own unique way and took the tie all the way off. Then she started unbuttoning my shirt. I didn't know what to say or do, so I let it happen. She kissed my now bare chest and scratched her hands gently down my back. I didn't want to get aroused, but I did. Hey, the wind can hit me in the right way and I get hard.

Be that as it may, I didn't want to do anything. Some old song popped into my head. "My mind is telling me no . . . but my body . . . " No, I wasn't going to let this happen. I wanted to get home and talk to Jen, if she was still awake.

Then Darcie unbuttoned my pants. I was still standing as she pulled them down below my knees. I stood there, and my penis betrayed me, transforming into stone. I needed to say something, to escape, to go home. But then she put it in her mouth.

I moaned, uncontrollably. Damn. She started using her hand too, blowing me and jerking me at the same time. I looked down, her auburn hair rubbing across my belly with the motions of her bobbing head. That was almost enough to make me push her away. But instead I rolled back my head, closed my eyes, and thought of something else. *Someone* else. You know what I pictured. A raven's dark hair, that thick chest, solid shoulders, the knee I so gently grazed that day, the hand he put on mine on the roller coaster. I pictured his gorgeous mouth opening wide to take me in the same way Darcie was right now.

And I just like that, in the instant it took to fantasize, I came as irrepressibly as I had moaned.

"Oh, gross, Nick! You're supposed to warn me!" Darcie was gagging, and when I opened my eyes, I started laughing hard. She kept gagging and I kept laughing. I think this may have been one of the funniest moments in my entire life. It was so wrong, but so hilarious. "What is wrong with you?"

I was laughing too hard to talk. "I . . . I . . . I'm sorry, I dunno . . ."

She went to the bathroom to clean up and I pulled up my pants. It's not exactly the way I imagined getting my first blow job. But let me tell you: it wasn't half bad.

Chapter Six

Of course I had to tell the guys all about my post-homecoming adventures with Darcie. We got together the next day to play some Call of Duty, and I let them in on my happy ending.

"You dawg!" Zack yelled. "How was it?"

"How do you think it was? It was awesome," I said.

"Man, none of my girls have ever wanted to do that," Asantà chimed in.

"I need to get a girlfriend," Jared mumbled, and we all laughed.

"It does have its perks," I said.

"Some tight ass perks," Toby added. "Like Asantà, none of my ladies ever wanted to do that. The most I've ever gotten was a handy, and they thought that was gross."

"I don't know why they think it's gross," I said. "It's hot." They looked at me weirdly then, and I said, "I mean, it's so hot for us. Why wouldn't they like that we like it?"

"Yeah, totally," Asantà said and gave a proud bro fist bump.

"I can't believe you," Jared said, still depressed over the lack of women in his life. "You suck."

"Nope. Darcie does." We all laughed.

It felt good to fit in.

*****

We had been playing for a few hours when Darcie texted, *Hi, baby. Wanna come over?*

I'm playing with the guys, I replied.

The way I play is more fun, she texted.

That's the truth.

Did you have fun last night?

U know I did.

Good. I love you.

Sigh. *Love ya too.*

I miss you.

Jesus, girl, I just saw you last night, I thought, but I texted, *miss u too* anyway. If I don't fully spell out "you," it somehow made me feel better. Love ya or miss u didn't feel quite as heavy.

Really?

Really.

K. Then come over.

We're in the middle of a game.

Come over when it's done.

I'll try if it's not too late.

Leave early enough so it's not too late.

K, I texted.

Promise?

I looked at the guys. It would be nice to have more stories to tell them. Maybe I'm not who I want to be. But who I want to be is someone who fits in. So, I'm kinda the guy I want to be. Maybe? So I texted back, *I promise. Give me one hour.*

Okay. I love you.

Sigh. *Luv ya too.*

And so I told the guys Darcie was begging for more. I even showed them the texts.

"You are such a playa!" Asantà said. "Go. Go, man. If I could get my wang sucked, I wouldn't be here playing these stupid video games."

"All right." I laughed. "See you tomorrow in school."

We bumped fists, and I went to Darcie's.

*****

"Perfect timing," she said. "My parents just left to go grocery shopping. That gives us at least an hour."

Now that I was here, I started wondering what the hell I was doing. I really didn't want to be doing this with Darcie. All I wanted, I guess, were some good stories to tell the guys. So I smiled and took a deep breath.

She grabbed my hand and pulled me towards her bedroom. This time she took off her shirt and laid down in bed. "Come here, on top of me."

I pulled my shirt over my head and did as she told me. Her tongue found my throat, and she moved to my neck. She bit softly, and then she did something that caught me off guard. She put her hands on my head and pushed me down. My head was over her chest, and so I kissed her breasts. I licked around the nipples, and she groaned and thrust her hips up and squeezed with her legs. I stayed here for a while. I did like boobs. Not licking them so much, but whatever. It's another story to tell the guys.

"You liked last night, yes?" she whispered in my ear.

"Definitely."

"Then you should return the pleasure." She pushed my head lower. She was wearing capris. I tried not to think, but I have to tell you: in this moment in my life, I had never been so frightened. DOWN THERE was not a place I had ever intended on going. No amount of fooling around could really prepare me for going DOWN THERE.

"C'mon, Nick, I wanna know what it feels like," she whispered and pulled my head toward her. She unbuttoned herself and slipped out of the capris.

Gross, nasty, disgusting. I won't do it. I *can't* do it. But how do I get out of this? And what do I say to Darcie? She'll get mad, and I might have to confess my secret. And then what do I tell the guys? I can picture the conversation now. *Yeah, guys, she wanted me to go down on her so I broke up with her. Gross, amiright?* No, they wouldn't understand, and the points I won with them would all be taken away. I wouldn't be looked up to, and I certainly wouldn't fit in.

So I told myself it will be like licking a lollipop. Close your eyes and picture yourself licking a nice cherry lollipop.

I lowered my head, cowering like a dog who lost a fight, and made my way to DOWN THERE. I took off her underwear, and Darcie started moaning. *Jesus, girl, I haven't even done anything yet.*

I saw a small patch of brown fuzz just above the DOWN THERE and then I closed my eyes and lowered my head. I found the lollipop. I started to lick it, gently. It had a strange smell, the juices from a fruit I had never tasted. It reminded me at first of a V8 fruit fusion drink, probably because I didn't like the taste of those. But I licked, and I had seen enough porn (although I usually focused on a very different private part during porn) to know I needed to do more with my tongue. Eyes closed, I thrust my tongue around. Then I let my fingers join the party, too. Darcie moaned louder. I started hoping we'd hear her front door slam and that her parents would come home. But no such luck, so I kept up my eyes shut tighter than ever.

Then she screamed. "Not that low!"

Oops.

If I'm going to do this right, I might have to take a peek. With great caution, I opened my eyes.

Dear God! It was frightening. I thought of a scene from *Star Wars*. You know that monstrous hole full of spikes and tentacles and danger? That's exactly what I thought of when I looked at the DOWN THERE on Darcie. I tried to close my eyes again, but the smell was getting stronger, the juices somehow wetter, and my stomach turned sick. I did the only thing I could think of.

"Oh my God! Did you hear that? I heard a door. Your parents must be home. Quick, get dressed. I'll run to the bathroom. I gotta clean up."

I ran out of her bedroom like a bat out of hell and dry heaved in the bathroom sink. Nothing came out, thankfully, but my throat felt raw and my stomach sick. *What the hell is wrong with me?* I stood staring in the mirror, trying to understand the reflection looking back at me.

You're such a pussy, I could hear the guys say.

I searched her bathroom cabinet, found some Listerine, and rinsed out my mouth.

Yeah, I guess I am, I told the guys in my head. *A pussy that doesn't want pussy.*

I stood there a minute longer. Her parents were not home, and by now, she'd have figured that out. Would she have known I was lying? Or could I convince her that I really thought I had heard a noise? Did it even matter?

Trembling like a bad puppy, I left the bathroom to face Darcie.

"Hey." She smiled. "Whatever you heard wasn't the door. Thank goodness. You gave me quite a scare."

Not half the terror you just put me through.

"Oh, good. Sorry. I . . . I guess I was paranoid."

"That's okay." She put her arms around me. "I still love you," she said and kissed me hard. Then she put her hand on my crotch. "It's my turn, now."

I tried to smile back. "I appreciate that, but I think I had one big scare already. I don't think we should risk it in case they do come home."

She looked at the time on her phone and replied, "We should have plenty of time. It's fine." Then she bent down on her knees and started to unzip my jeans.

"No, really, you don't have to. Thank you, but let's not rush it."

She stood up and looked me hard in the eyes. "I can't imagine too many guys who would turn that down."

"Yeah, I guess. Sorry but I don't want us to get in trouble."

She frowned, studying me with her eyes. I looked the other way in case somehow she could see my truth. "Okay."

"So, maybe I should head out?"

"If you think so."

"I can call you when I get home," I told her.

"If you want to."

"Okay, good night." I leaned in and kissed her. She kept her mouth closed, kissing me back a little but not with her usual forceful passion.

"Bye," I said again. It was the first time I could remember her not saying "I love you," telling me to call her, or kissing me so long that I had to break and let go.

It was exactly what I had been wanting. But Darcie not doing any of those things made me feel a new weirdness. Something was changing, and even if I had wanted her to act more like this Darcie standing in front of me, I wasn't sure I liked it very much after all. I was happy and sad all at the same time again. Back on the roller coaster, spinning through a loop I didn't understand.

Chapter Seven

The next exciting event to happen at school was the Halloween dance. It had been several weeks since homecoming, and Darcie and I were somehow still together. She had distanced herself, though. She still texted good night, but she didn't call or ask me to call. We still hung out at least once a week, but we only kissed if we did begin to make out at all. It was a strange dichotomy: she distanced herself yet still hung on, perhaps some weird dynamic of a teenage relationship I didn't understand.

I never told the guys about the night she made me go DOWN THERE. They asked if we had gone any further, and I said no. They of course had some crude reply like, "Boy, you best be gettin' that dick in her while you can!"

At home, Jen was being super cool in that she hadn't brought up our conversation again or told our parents about it. She seemed much wiser than you'd think she'd be at her age. Her strategy seemed to be that she'd ask if I wanted to hang or she'd just sit with me quietly watching a movie. She hadn't pressed the issue any more.

As for Derek? I looked for him in the stands of every football game every Friday night. It became the main reason I attended those damn games. Since I hadn't found him online after we played Mayville High, I had hoped he had attended with a friend from a different school and that maybe he'd show up again. But he hadn't, or at least I never saw him. Sometimes you want something so bad you can taste it, people say. The memory of Derek hit me sporadically, filling me with the yin and yang of happy sadness I was getting accustomed to feeling. Sometimes I thought for sure I'd see him again, and I told myself to be patient, to not lose hope, to use the time to think of the perfect thing to say whenever I did run into him again. More often, however, I told myself to stop thinking about him because the chances of me running into him were probably about the same as getting struck by lightning. And if I did see him, I reminded myself of how he crumpled up the note I gave him outside of the bus, the note with my name and number. I pictured him throwing it on the ground, turning around, and walking away. Certainly, he never thought of me and had moved on. I should get used to having my dreams crushed.

A happy hope or a sad reality: either way, it was vicious.

The Halloween dance was tonight, and since it featured a costume contest, I thought it would make for a good distraction. The dance also marked a good time of year. We'd start our basketball season in November, so life was about to get crazy busy, and that's the way I liked it. The busier I was, the less time I had to think about everything else. I had talked the guys into going as characters from *Game of Thrones*. They weren't so big on reading; I was the only guy who truly read for fun in our group. But I made them watch the first season, and as soon as people's heads started getting chopped off and women's boobs flashed on screen, they became huge fans. We had talked Darcie into dressing up as Daenerys. I was going as Jon Snow, Jared was going to be Hodor since he was the tallest of us, Toby was dressing as Joffrey, Asantà dressed as Drogon the dragon ("he's the blackest thing in the show!" he said), and Zack, the shortest of us, was going as a black Tyrion.

"So this means Darcie gets to pet me and feed me all night, right?" Asantà asked.

"In your dreams," she said.

"C'mon, you can't see Dani giving Jon Snow head, can you? Give someone else some love tonight," he taunted her. I laughed, thinking about how the series ended.

She snapped me a dirty look. We had never talked about what I had or had not told the guys, but after Asantà's bad joke, she must have had a pretty good idea.

"Maybe I will," she said but kept her focus on me. I shrugged and mouthed "what?"

She shook her head and led us into the dance, which was being held at the Worthless High gymnasium. The student council had decorated and sponsored a DJ for the night. The decorations were actually pretty cool: lots of hanging skeletons, carved pumpkins, spider webs, and everyone was dressed up. We were initially worried that people would have a "too cool" attitude to come in costume, but there were plenty of clowns, serial killers, and semi-slutty girls (the school had enforced a dress code, but of course many girls pushed it as much as possible).

The first person to catch my eye was Steve, the only out gay guy in our school who ran the gay-straight student alliance. He had his normal crew of freshman girls hanging by him. He dressed as Maleficent. Of course he's a girl. I didn't intend to think cruel thoughts about Steve, but I couldn't help but be pissed off and annoyed by him. Sure, part of the reason I felt that way was jealousy: he was who he was and he didn't give a damn about fitting in. But here's the thing: I don't feel like a girl stuck in a guy's body. I'm a dude who knows that I like dudes. And then I look around, trying to figure out where I will fit in, and there's nobody. Maybe this is why the rest of us don't come out. There are like a thousand people at this school. Steve is clearly not the only gay guy. But it's damn hard to come out when no one who is out is quite like you.

I hear my own thoughts, and I know I sound like an asshole and a coward.

I suppose that's because I am an asshole and a coward.

I push the thoughts from my mind. I'm going to enjoy this damn Halloween dance.

But I catch Steve looking at me. He waves and smiles. I nod back. I wonder if there is such a thing as gaydar and if he knows I'm probably more like him than the guys I hang with.

The music begins to play, and it's a much needed distraction from my thoughts. The first song of course is Michael Jackson's "Thriller." I'm not a dancer, but I join a circle that's formed around a bunch of guys doing the "Thriller" dance. Asantà joins in. Man, he's got some moves. He motions for Darcie to join, and we laugh at Dani and her dragon doing the "Thriller" moves. The music is loud, and the vibrations feel nice. It's so loud, you can't even think, and it feels fantastic. I wonder if this is why clubs are so popular: from the noise to the vibrations, not a thought can enter your mind. The body moves and the mind takes a vacation.

The song ends, and Zack and I get a drink. The other guys are still dancing and Darcie seems to be enjoying herself, which is perfectly fine with me.

"This is one of those times I wish this were some high school movie where'd someone spike the punch," Zack said, pouring a drink.

"Yeah, me too."

"Maybe we could get some booze tonight. We got full practices next week. One big party before we start a week of doubles."

"Where could we get it?"

"Jared has an older brother. Let's ask him," Zack said.

"Cool." I've never been drunk. I've had a couple of beers, but I've never felt the way people seem to feel on TV, stumbling and mumbling like obnoxious zombies. "I'm game."

Zack rejoined the group on the dance floor, and I stayed behind by the drink and snack table. It's nice to watch sometimes. Most students had gathered in little circles around the gym floor, not really dancing but hanging with their own groups. A few people kept on grooving, Asantà and Darcie two of them.

"I don't know if I'd let my girlfriend dance with another guy all night," a voice called out to me.

I turned and it was Steve.

"Hey," I said. "We're all just friends."

"Not you and Darcie," he stated.

"No, not me and Darcie."

"So why aren't you out there dancing with her?" Steve asked.

"I'm not much of a dancer."

"Hmmm," he mumbled.

I really didn't want to talk to him. But the way he said the "hmm" bothered me. Of course, my mind jumped right to paranoia. Is he judging me for being gay and not being able to dance?

"What do you mean?" I asked.

"What do you mean what do I mean?"

"You said 'hmm.' What does that mean?"

He looked me up and down, his Maleficent horns almost stabbing me in the face.

"I just thought you might be a good dancer. You look like you'd be a good dancer," he said.

"Well, I'm not."

"Okay. You don't have to be defensive. I'm only making conversation."

He left then, and my stupid paranoid mind was sure that he knew exactly who I was and what I was hiding. I watched him return to his posse of freshman girls and dance far better than I ever could. Maybe he really was a girl trapped in a guy's body. He sure swayed like one.

Toby and Jared came over to get some drinks. Zack, Asantà, and Darcie were now dancing to an LMFAO song.

"Dude, I texted my bro," Jared said. "He replied 'it's about time you get some hair on your chest.' Ha! He's going to get us a couple of cases of beer and a bottle of Jack."

"Jack?" I asked.

"Jack Daniels. It's whiskey. It's supposed to get you stupid drunk fast."

"This is gonna rock!" Toby said. "We just have to find a place to do it. My parents are home. Yours?"

"Yeah, mine will be home," I said.

"Asantà has the whole basement to himself. His parents are upstairs, but there's a bathroom in the basement. That may be our best bet," Toby said.

"Yeah, let's check with him," Jared said. He was so tall he had to look down to talk to me. "You okay, man? You've been over here since the first song?"

Fortunately, his Hodor costume made me laugh, and I said, "Yeah, man, I'm fine. Just not much of a dancer, you know."

"K. Cool. We gonna party tonight!" Jared cheered and they left to talk with Asantà.

My eyes were drawn to Steve, though. I kept watching him dance with his female friends. Happiness poured from his body and smile, and I couldn't help but feel envious at how comfortable he appeared. He caught me staring twice, and I quickly looked away. Yeah, I thought, booze would be good. This punch isn't doing anything for me. But I had several cups, enough to need to go to the bathroom already.

I left the drink table and went into the men's room. It was completely empty, too early in the dance for most people to need to pee, I guess. I went to a urinal and put my arms up against the wall, my head into my arms, and did my business. The music was softer in here, and my thoughts came rushing back all over again. It's weird. When I'm alone, I get bored and want to be with other people. Then sometimes I'm with other people and I just want to be alone again.

The bathroom door opened, and I snapped my head back, flushed the urinal, and washed my hands. I didn't look up to see who it was. I didn't care. I wasn't alone anymore, so I had no reason to linger in the stinky men's room.

"Hey again," a voice called.

It was Steve. I turned around and said politely, "Hey again."

"You okay?" he asked.

"Yeah, fine. Why?"

"Sorry. Don't need to snap at me. I know we're not close. I just saw that you've been hanging a lot by yourself. So I thought I'd ask. That's all."

"It's not necessary. I'm fine."

"Okay, okay." Steve put his hands up in retreat.

I looked closer at Steve and his Maleficent costume. Behind the mask and the makeup, he was pretty cute. A round face, slightly overweight, but he had nice blue eyes and a kind smile. *What the hell am I thinking?*

"I'm sorry," I told him. "I didn't mean to snap. It's nice that you care."

He smiled at me. I thought that beneath the costume and the theatrics, he must have had a kind heart and soul. A much nicer person than me anyway. The song changed out in the gym. It was some Nicki Minaj song that made the crowd cheer and scream.

"It's okay. Wow. And the crowd goes wild!" Steve said at the song change.

"This one's not really my style."

"Oh, I love it! So what is your style then?" He smiled at me again.

"I'm a rock guy. Loud drums, rough guitar, and a guy who can scream," I said.

"I like a guy who can scream, too." Steve grinned.

I laughed and found myself relaxing. "Yeah, that's not what I meant."

"What did you think I meant?" he asked coyly.

I giggled awkwardly. "Nothing."

He gave me another "hmmm." And then he said, "You're kinda rough on the outside. I get that you like rock. But I'm also guessing you have a few songs on your iPod you don't tell anyone about. Maybe some Katy Perry. Or Gaga. Maybe Britney or Miley?" he asked.

The truth is I had a few songs from all of those artists, and no, I didn't tell anyone about that.

"Not really my style," I lied.

"Hmm. Okay."

"All right, maybe one or two of them." I smiled.

"Ha! See, music is weird like that. We'll hate on artists that it's cool to hate on publicly, and then we'll secretly listen and dance to their songs when no one's watching."

"You don't strike me as having too many secrets," I said.

"Just because my heart is on my sleeve doesn't mean I don't have plenty of things I don't tell others."

That kind of shocked me. Is that weird? I looked at someone like Steve who appears completely comfortable with his sexuality and figured that he must be open about everything. It never occurred to me that he may have secrets, too.

"What kind of things?"

"Well, I haven't told any of my friends that there's one guy at this dance who I think is absolutely gorgeous." He smiled.

"Who would that be?" I wondered.

"You're a bit naïve. I like that."

I had to think about that for a moment. "Oh," I said, blushing. "Really?"

"Really. But I don't know if he's like me. Or if he'd even *like* me."

"Oh," I said, losing my smile.

"I'm sorry. Now I've embarrassed you." He started to walk away.

"Steve," I said. He turned around, those ridiculous Maleficent horns making me smile.

It's Halloween. We should be whoever we want to be and do whatever we want to do, I thought.

I grabbed Steve and kissed him.

"Woah," he pulled back. "Really?"

"Sorry. I don't know what I'm doing."

"No, you just caught me off guard. Like really off guard. But, uh, let's try it again." He grabbed me this time and kissed me. He was a good kisser, and I sure had an adrenaline rush hiding here in the bathroom where anyone could walk in.

It was a long, passionate kiss, and I realized this was my first kiss with a guy. It may not have been the guy I dreamed about, but it was nice. It fit. Kissing Darcie never quite fit, and even if I wasn't totally into Steve, there was something about his mouth and his smell that felt natural to me, the way lips should feel when kissed.

Then we heard the door open and I pulled my face away hurriedly. We were still close though, my arm lingering around his waist, his remaining around my neck.

That's when Asantà saw us. His eyes bulged, he threw up his hands and mouthed a "woah." He looked at me with shock and surprise and then turned around and left the bathroom.

"Shit," I said.

Steve looked at me sadly. "Yeah. I think you're in for an interesting night."

"You don't know the half of it."

"I can guess. Here, give me your phone," he said.

"Why?"

"I'm not expecting anything crazy. I'm just giving you my number. If things get weird tonight, call or text me, okay?"

I handed him my phone. "Oh, okay. Thanks."

"No problem. I guess I'll let you get to your friends." He paused and stared, and I'm not sure if he wanted to kiss me again or not. Instead he hugged me.

One moment I'm criticizing Steve in my head. Another moment I'm kissing him. All the while, he's just a good guy with a much bigger heart than I have. It made me feel like shit.

"Good luck," Steve said and left.

He must see right through me, and let's face it—he deserves better than me. So does Darcie. So does Derek.

How do I get better? I want to be better.

I took a deep breath.

I knew the answer.

I turned around and looked at my reflection in the mirror. "It starts with the truth," I said. "God help me." And I left the bathroom to return to my friends.

Chapter Eight

The post-Halloween party plans were in the works. Jared would pick up the alcohol from his brother, and we'd meet at Asantà's house. He said his parents would be asleep anyway, and that as long as we weren't too loud, we'd be fine in the basement.

The rest of the dance was incredibly long. I felt like I was watching one of *The Hobbit* movies again, wondering when the hell this would all be over. Asantà didn't say anything to me. He looked at me a few times in a mysterious "I'm still trying to figure you out" look. We were never alone though, which I suppose was good, as I wasn't even sure I wanted to talk to him about it. I was hoping he'd undergo serious memory loss.

Zack asked me before we left, "So are you gonna invite your girl?"

"I don't know. What if Asantà's parents do come down? Would it be worse if there was a girl there, too?" I asked.

"Maybe. Or at least getting her out the next morning. Probably best not to invite her."

That was one plus for the night.

Before we left, I talked to Darcie outside. "So I'm spending the night with the guys at Asantà's."

"Okay," she said. "I hope you have a good time." She wasn't exactly cold, but she definitely wasn't warm. I didn't even kiss her good night, and there was no "I love you" or "call me" either. I felt a bit depressed by this, mainly because it was yet another thing I'd have to deal with. Eventually. Right now it was about a party with the guys. And hoping that Asantà doesn't bring up what he saw in the bathroom at the Halloween dance.

We all ran home first to tell our parents and grab a sleeping bag plus a change of clothes. "Mom, can I please stay at Asantà's tonight? All the guys are crashing there."

She looked at me with that motherly concern but said, "Okay. You're on double practices next week for basketball right?"

"Yeah."

"Don't stay up too late then. You'll want your energy for next week." I'm convinced this was her polite way of saying don't drink. I had never come home hung-over before, so I don't know why she may have worried that this would be the time it would happen. Maybe because it was Halloween, and on Halloween anything can happen.

We met in Asantà's basement. He looked at me curiously, but he hadn't said anything. Zack and Toby were anxious and excited. Jared was the last to arrive, but he came through. He had a 30 pack of beer and a bottle of Jack Daniels.

We poured a shot of Jack for each of us first. "To getting trashed," Jared said.

"Our first time should be together. Just the five of us," Zack said. "To best friends."

I looked at Asantà and hoped he felt the same. I repeated what Zack said, looking right at Asantà to be sure he'd understand: "To best friends." We clinked our shot glasses, and Asantà even nodded at me.

"Ooh, man," Toby yelled. "It burns!"

"My brother says that's how we get hair on our chests!" Jared laughed.

"You have enough hair on your ass," Zack said.

We laughed and poured another shot. "To the team," Asantà said. "To kicking ass this season." We raised our glasses again and did a second shot.

"Damn," I chocked. "That's terrible. Why do people drink this?"

"I'm guessing we'll know why in a few minutes," Toby said.

"I don't feel anything yet. One more before the beer?" I asked. I wanted to get drunk. Sloppy, get-these thoughts-out-of-my-head drunk.

"You got it, boss," Jared said. "What should we drink to this time?"

Asantà raised his glass and said, "To honesty." He looked at me, and I frowned. Was he mad at me?

Zack joked, "We're always honest, bro. I got a better one. To tits and ass!"

"To blow jobs!" Jared said.

"To pussy!" Toby added.

"To my nasty ass friends," I said. We all clinked shot glasses again and drank. It went down a little easier the third time.

"Okay, my bro says to take it easy on the Jack," Jared said. "Let's switch to beer. What about a drinking game?"

"Yeah. Let's bust out the Call of Duty. Every time you're shot, you drink," Asantà suggested.

"Perfect," Zack said. "I'm gonna kill all you fuckers."

*****

You can imagine it didn't take long for us to get drunk. It was about an hour into our drinking game that we had to stop. The room was already spinning for me, but we were laughing so hard it didn't matter.

"Enough of this game," Toby said. "I can't focus any longer."

"Okay, so now what?" Zack asked.

"Cards?" Jared said.

"How about we go old school?" Asantà requested. "Truth or dare."

"I haven't played that since I was a kid," Zack said.

"So it will be perfect." Asantà looked right at me when he said this. I was starting to feel nervous and drank my beer a little quicker.

"Okay, bro, you asked for it, you're up first," Jared told Asantà. "Truth or dare?"

"Truth," he said.

"We need a good one guys," Toby said. "How about this? If you could have any girlfriend from any of the chicks at school, who would it be?"

Asantà looked at me hard. "Truth is . . . I would choose Darcie."

"Ooooh!" all three of the other guys yelped and looked at me. "That's not cool, man!" Zack said.

"What do you think about that, Nick?" Toby asked.

My head was floating. I didn't know what to think. I had an answer, somewhere. And then it left me. I was trying to find something serious and something funny. And then I said, "Maybe he just wants a threesome!"

The others giggled, and I relaxed a bit when Asantà laughed, too.

"Okay, my turn to ask," Asantà said. "Nick. Truth or dare."

"Dare," I said.

He shook his head. "Okay, I dare you to kiss someone in this room."

"Gross, dude!" Jared yelled. "That's not a dare you give someone when it's all guys."

"Yeah, c'mon, Asantà. Be cool," Toby said.

"I am being cool," he said sternly. "Nick's up for it. Kiss any guy in this room."

"First you want a threesome, and now you want me to kiss someone?" I asked. The other three cackled. This time, Asantà did not. "What happens if I don't?"

"Yeah," Toby said. "What's the punishment? A shot?"

"Two shots in a row," Asantà said. My stomach churned. I couldn't handle that much without spewing chunks.

"You want me to puke in your room?" I asked. He didn't fold. "Okay, then who?" I tried to be silly. "Which of you sexy beasts can I put my lips on?"

They all looked away. I really thought about choosing Asantà, but I also worried that he might punch me.

"Zack!" I yelled. "You are so cute. Get over here."

"Fuck you, man. This game is stupid! I'll do your shots."

"Okay, if that's what you want."

Zack was already pouring a shot of more Jack.

"Then it's my turn to ask," I said.

"No," Asantà said. "Zack can take your shots, but since you didn't do the dare, then you have to take a truth first."

"That sounds fair," Jared mumbled. "Truth to Nick! What should we ask?"

"Have you gone down on Darcie?" Toby asked.

"Have you had sex with her?" Zack chocked in between shots.

"No, let me, guys," Asantà said. "You guys asked me if there's any chick at school I would be with. I want to ask Nick if there's any person other than Darcie that he'd rather be with. And if so, who?"

"That sounds like two truths," I slurred, trying to argue.

"I'll rephrase," he said. "Not including Darcie, tell us about one person—any person—you would *honestly* like to be with."

Suddenly, the fun of drinking had diminished. I felt all of the sickness and none of the pleasure. "Asantà . . ." I started to plead but the other guys were all watching. "I . . . I don't know." Then I shook my head and looked at him, trying to make him understand that this was not cool. This was not how I wanted to do this.

"Answer the question," he said.

"Yeah, c'mon, Nick, why won't you answer the question?" Jared asked.

"I don't want to answer the question, guys."

"What's wrong?" Toby asked. "Fuckin' just make something up then."

"Okay, fine. I'd pick . . . Asantà's mom."

The guys were quiet for a moment and then all burst out laughing. Asantà looked at me and shook his head again but he smiled. "Piss break," I said. I wanted to do something to break up the game and talk to Asantà alone.

"Me first!" Zack shouted and sprinted to the bathroom. Jared laughed so hard he fell backwards and Toby followed suit. While they were on the floor laughing and Zack was in the bathroom, I took this moment to say something to Asantà.

"Please, dude. Let me explain. But just to you. Not here like this. Not in front of everybody like this. I can explain, but it's harder than you think."

As our leader of the group, Asantà's opinion was golden. I tried to read him, and he didn't look hateful. He looked hurt, perhaps because I simply hadn't been honest with him. I prayed that was the case.

"Okay," he said.

"Okay?"

"Yeah, okay."

Now I just had to hope the others would pass out before me or Asantà. "Okay, guys, who wants another shot?

*****

It was sometime in the middle of the night that Zack threw up in the bathroom. The sounds were disgusting enough that I almost puked from listening to him. Around the same time, Jared and Toby passed out. The bottle of Jack was empty, and there were only a few beers left in the case. Although I was seeing triple of everything and the room felt like a never-ending spinning disco, I managed to stay awake. And so had Asantà.

He looked pretty drunk, too. He'd belch and giggle and then look up at me, remembering what had happened, and frown. Now is as good of a time as any, I thought.

"Hey," I said, scooting closer to him on the floor. "I'm sorry you walked in and saw that. You know, at the dance."

"Yeah, so am I." He looked down and took another sip of his beer.

"Why are you sorry? And why are you mad?" I was drunk enough to challenge him.

"You've lied to me all these years. We've been friends since we started playing ball as freshmen. You're my main guy on the court, ya know? And now I feel like I don't even know you."

"So." I tried to find the right words to say. "So you're not mad that I was with a dude? You're mad because I never told you about it?"

"Bro, I don't give a fuck who you want to fuck. But you've been livin' a lie and that pisses me off."

I had to think about that for a moment. And then I knew exactly what I needed to ask him. "So, let me you ask you this. Are you gay?"

"Fuck no!" he yelled.

"That's what I thought you'd say. No, I mean, that's how I thought you'd say it. Don't you see? You say 'fuck no' like it's a bad thing. Don't you get it? You still react like it's not . . . not cool or not normal." I took a deep breath and was hoping that I was making sense. *Was I slurring my words?* I sounded fine in my own head, but I wanted to make sure to say this right. "And you expect me to be honest when that's how you react?"

Asantà took another drink from his beer, finished it, and grabbed two more. "Here," he said. "We drink till it's gone."

"Dude, I've never told anyone about this part of me before." I caught my own lie, unintentional as it was, and corrected myself. *If I'm going to start being honest, I need to be completely honest.* "That's not true. I told my sister, Jen. She kinda . . . tricked me, I guess. Not really a trick, but you know? I don't know. She just knew somehow."

"Your parents know?"

"I haven't told them."

"No one else but your sis?"

"No one else."

"What about Darcie?"

"She doesn't know."

"Well I figured that." He laughed. "But why are you going out with her?"

"I don't know." I paused for a while and we drank our beers. "She liked me. I thought having a girlfriend would help me fit in."

"Do you like Steve?" he asked.

"No. That was a weird thing you walked in on. He was nice and I think he figured me out and I . . . I dunno. It was all very spontaneous. I'd never kissed a guy before."

"Oh."

I'm sure some of this was the alcohol, but Asantà seemed to relax a lot more. Then he asked, "Do you like anyone?"

"I did. But no one you know."

"So, you're not like secretly in love with one of us?" He gestured sloppily at the other guys in the basement, now all passed out.

"No." I laughed. "You're my best friends. I'm sorry I never told you before. I was just scared that you wouldn't be my friends anymore."

Asantà sighed. "That's stupid. We will always be your friends. At least I will. I'm sorry, too. I don't know why I was pissed." He paused and sighed, the booze taking more and more of an effect. "I hate liars. But I get it. I'm sorry I said 'fuck no' when you asked if I was gay. I didn't mean it to sound like that."

"I know. But I worry there are gonna be a lot of people who do mean it to sound exactly like that."

"I got your back, bro." He held up his fist. I bumped it and smiled.

"Thanks, man."

"I'm your best friend. And I'll be your best man if you ever marry a bro in the future. It don't matter."

I knew what was about to happen, and I blame it all on this goddamn stupid alcohol. All of the booze combined with Asantà's acceptance: I wasn't sure if I expected that or not. And then he goes and says he'd be my best man? I couldn't help it. I started crying. And once I started the tears kept on rolling. I couldn't stop. I felt like an idiot. I didn't want to cry in front of him, I wanted to stop it right now, but I was powerless.

He scooted closer to me and put an arm around me.

"It'll be okay."

I couldn't talk. The fucking tears wouldn't stop. I tried to open my mouth and say something, but all I felt was drool and snot beginning to run out my nose. I was a hot mess.

"You cry, dude. Nothin' wrong with it. No one here, not me, not no one, knows what it's like to keep so much inside you and for God knows how long. You let it all out."

He held me even closer and I sobbed on his shoulder. I don't know if this would have happened without all the booze, but regardless of the fact that we were drunk, it was the nicest thing a friend had ever done for me.

"You have no idea . . ." I choked out. "I always thought I could fit in or I could be myself. I never thought it could be both."

"You remember Asantà's got your back. Ain't no haters gonna hate on my bro. Got that?"

I wiped the tears from my face with my sleeve. "Got it," I said. We leaned back against the wall and just sat there. His arm around me, my tears and my pain fading away, like the darkness of night vanishing behind the sun. We passed out, just two friends. Two best friends.

Chapter Nine

Hello, hangover. The sun was coming through the windows in Asantà's basement, and my head felt like it was going to explode. My body felt like I had belly flopped into a pool with no water and slammed on a concrete floor.

"You boys," Asantà's mom yelled from upstairs. "I'm making pancakes!"

Asantà woke up slowly, his head still against the wall where we had passed out. "No offense to your mom," I said, "but that makes me want to puke."

"No worries. Me, too," he said.

"I feel like I've been hit by a train." Jared stretched and woke up on the couch across the room. "Oh, Jesus."

"This sucks," Toby added, waking up. "And you know we have our first double practice tomorrow. Before school at six and after school at three. I think I'm gonna have to take a sick day."

"Don't even think about it," Asantà told him. "We just need . . . A lot of water today. We'll be okay."

"What's wrong with you guys?" Zack asked. Coming out of the bathroom, he looked fully awake and rested. "I feel fine."

"That's cuz you puked it all up last night in my damn bathroom," Asantà said.

"Yeah, sorry about that."

"You better clean it up."

"I did. I mean." Zack stopped and looked back at the toilet, "Uh, I will."

Everyone was slow to wake, and Toby looked over at Asantà and me and asked, "You guys okay? You both kinda got weird last night."

Asantà looked at me and nodded. Then he said to Toby, "We're cool, man. It was the booze or something. Weird how it changes your mood, isn't it?"

"Yeah, cool."

Asantà whispered in my ear. "I'm not saying anything. You tell them when you're ready. But they'll be cool, and you should be honest with your bros, all right?"

"I will. Just not now. Not hung-over like this."

"Yeah, I hear ya," he agreed and rubbed his forehead.

"Baby, do you and your friends want some pancakes?" his mom called down to us again.

Asantà looked around the room at our sick, pale faces. Zack poked his head out of the bathroom and said, "I'd love some!"

After giving Zack a dirty look, Asantà yelled upstairs, "No, mom, we can't do carbs today. It's coach's rule."

"Oh, you should have told me. Now what will I do with all these pancakes?"

The guys laughed and Zack said, "That was mean. I'd have taken some."

"You're not enjoying my mama's food when I can't enjoy it," Asantà said.

Sick, hung-over, pale: It didn't matter. I laughed. It felt good to be alive this morning. Pain, after all, may be most unpleasant, but it is at least a constant reminder that we are fully alive.

*****

Later Jared gave me a ride home, and a few minutes into the drive, I told him, "You're gonna have to pull over." I really thought I'd make it through this Sunday without puking. I was wrong.

"What? Why?"

"Do you want me to hurl in your car?"

"Oh, shit!" He pulled over quickly then. The vomit started coming out of my mouth the moment the passenger door opened. I hurled five or six times at the corner of some side street. An old man came out of the closest house. He could have been deaf, but my projectiles could have been heard across the state.

"Hey, you! Hey, boy! What are you doing?"

I replied with a thorough cleansing of my guts.

"I'm going to call the police. That is disgusting!" the old man yelled.

"Shut up, dude. He's sick, not a criminal." Jared staggered from the car to see if I needed help. "You okay, man?"

"Why does vomit bring out all the tears and snot, too?" I replied wiping my nose and eyes with my sleeve. This poor sleeve had seen a lot of action in the past day.

"Gross!"

"I'm okay. I think. Take me home."

"Gladly."

I made it the rest of the way without puking, but I should have made Jared pull over before we got to my house because the minute we arrived, I felt sick again.

"Thanks for the ride," I told him and ran to the back of the house. Dad's poor bushes got some unwanted fertilizer.

I tried to sneak into the house. I certainly didn't want my parents seeing me this way. I almost made it to my room before I heard a "hey."

It was only Jen. "Oh gosh, you look terrible, Nick! What's wrong?"

"Shhh. Nothing. I need to get in my room."

Jen followed me into my bedroom. I took off my shirt and threw it to the side and fell in bed. "What is wrong with you?" she asked.

"Don't tell Mom or Dad. Please. And whatever you do, don't ever drink. It's the most terrible thing in the world."

"Drink what?"

"Alcohol, stupid."

"You didn't! Oh, Mom and Dad are gonna be so mad!"

"You're not gonna tell them. Because you're the best sister in the world, remember?"

She may have been cool with me being gay. That's just who I was. But she was not cool about me getting drunk. Because that was just a stupid thing to do.

"What were you thinking?"

"I didn't want to think. You're too young to understand."

"Hmmm." She smiled. "So what do I get if I don't tell?"

"You rat!" I threw a pillow at her. "Fine. What do you want?"

"Gee, let me think!" She was dancing around the room now, happy as could be. "What could you give me that I would want?"

"Make up your mind, brat, and leave me alone. I do not feel well."

"I can see that!"

She danced around my bed and started singing, "What do I want, what do I want, what do I want!"

I buried my head in my blankets. "Please, Jen! Please be quiet and let me sleep."

"I got it!" she yelled extra loud on purpose. "I want three things. Are you ready?"

"Ugh," I grunted at her.

"First, I want your next week's allowance."

"I never knew you were so greedy."

"Second," she continued, ignoring me, "I get to use your room to watch TV the rest of the month. Mom's on some stupid cooking show binge, and it's *so* boring."

"Fine. What else?"

"Last, and you have to promise . . . you promise I get all three of these things?"

"You haven't told me what the last one is yet."

"You have to promise first. Or I get to tell. Your choice."

"Fine, I promise. My allowance, my TV, and whatever your third thing is."

"My final request is that you tell Mom and Dad before Christmas."

"Tell them what?"

"You know what."

I sat up in bed. "Jen, I don't know . . . why would you want that?"

"I want a good Christmas. The best Christmas. You know it's my favorite holiday! And it doesn't feel right. I want them to know what I know."

"I don't know, Jen."

"You already promised."

"That's not fair!"

"Fine. I'll go get Mom and Dad now and tell them you have a drinking problem."

"Okay, okay," I said. Sure, perhaps them finding out I got drunk for the first time wouldn't be nearly as big as me telling them I was gay. But that would mean dealing with them right now. No matter how big the problem, it always seems better to choose whatever option gives you the most time to deal with it.

"You promised, now. Don't forget. And *before* Christmas. So we can enjoy it. Not on Christmas, okay?"

"I promise. Just let me sleep. And if Mom or Dad ask, tell them I'm sleeping so I can rest up for double practice tomorrow."

"Okay. Good night, stupid."

"Get out of my room, dummy." She giggled all the way out. Part of me thought that after telling Asantà that I should definitely be able to tell Mom and Dad. They have to support me right? Asantà had a choice. But if nothing else, by that time, it would be too late for Jen to rat me out for drinking if I broke my promise. Promises do get broken.

*****

"Honey, dinner is ready. You awake?" Mom poked her head in my bedroom door.

"Yeah, Mom. I'm getting up. Thanks."

"Can I come in?"

I hoped I didn't look like complete shit. "I guess," I said.

"You feeling okay?"

"Yeah, we just didn't sleep much last night. That's all. And we've got our double practices starting tomorrow. Bright and early."

"I bet you didn't sleep much," she said, sitting on my bed. She ran her hand through my hair. "Nick, I have to tell you something."

"What's that?"

"You smell really bad."

"What?"

"How much did you have to drink last night?"

"Just a little."

"Smells like you drank an entire bar and all the vomit that may have resulted after."

I sat up in bed and tried not to breathe in her general direction.

"I'm sorry. Are you mad?"

"Hmm." She sighed and looked at me closely with that terrible parental look of disappointment that could break the spirit of the world's most devoted spy. "Look, I know kids will drink. I'm not stupid. I'm disappointed that *my son* is now one of those kids."

"I'm never drinking again, I promise."

"That's what they all say."

"Am I in trouble?"

She paused for a moment and took a deep breath. "I want you to spend a half hour looking at yourself in the mirror. The way you look now, I'm hoping that will be enough punishment and a big enough reminder of what can happen when you drink. We will have a follow up talk on this. Lots of things can go wrong when you party like that, and I need to know that you know how to be safe."

"I was safe, I promise. Just stupid. Are you gonna tell Dad?"

"I think stupid and safe may be mutually exclusive. No, I won't tell Dad, at least not tonight. But yes, eventually. If you don't want him to know now, you best shower before you come downstairs."

"Okay."

"I love you, Nick. Your Dad and I both love you. And we want to see you happy and healthy, always. You understand?"

"I understand. And I love you, too." It felt good to say that. I hadn't said "I love you" and meant it in a long time.

"Okay, get showered, come get some dinner, and then back to bed. You've got quite the week ahead of you, huh?"

"Yeah, there's a lot going on."

*****

The night wasn't quite complete. I don't think I had ever wished for a day to be over and for the normalcy of school to begin. That evening, I got a text from Darcie. *Call me tonight. Please. It's important.* I wanted to ignore it. You know I did.

But I called her anyway.

"Hey, babe," Darcie answered. "How are you?"

"Okay. Tired. You?"

She sighed. "Yeah, the same I guess."

"So, what's up?"

"Does something have to be up for you to call me?" she asked.

"Course not."

"Good. But yeah something's up."

"What is it?"

"How much do you trust Asantà?"

That was a strange question. Where was this coming from? Considering everything that happened last night, there was only one answer: "With my life."

"Really?"

"Yeah, he's my best friend."

"Oh." Silence. What was she thinking? What was going on?

"Did something happen?"

"I don't know," she mumbled. "He said something to me last night before we left the dance. I didn't know if I should tell you or not, but it's been bothering me all day."

"What did he say?"

"It was one of the last songs of the night. We were dancing. He leaned in close and said, 'if anything ever happens between you and Nick, I want you to know you're beautiful.' What do you think he meant by that?"

"Oh, wow. I dunno." Now lots of thoughts shot through my head. Was he saying this to protect her? Clearly, this took place after he saw me kiss Steve. But then later at his house when we did Truth or Dare, he did say if there was one girl he could be with it would be Darcie. Did he have real feelings for her?

"Have you told him anything you haven't told me?"

"What do you mean?"

"Like about us. I have to be honest. It sounds like he knows something I don't. And that if something were to happen to us . . . I'm still beautiful? C'mon. If you're his best friend, that has to mean something to you. Are we okay?"

That was the question with the million dollar answer, wasn't it? I did like Darcie. I didn't like her in a girlfriend way, but here we were: boyfriend and girlfriend. This couldn't go on forever, but I didn't know when or how to end it. It wasn't a priority tonight. Hydration and sleep were my only priorities tonight.

"You're taking too long to answer," she said. "That tells me everything I need to know."

"Wait, Darcie . . . We're okay. I mean, I don't know. It's complicated."

"Relationships shouldn't be complicated, even if Facebook has an option for them. If it's complicated, it's time to move on."

"Are you telling me you want to move on?"

"Are you telling me we're complicated?"

"Look. I like you. Really. There are some things we should talk about, I guess. But not tonight. Not like this on the phone. What about next Friday? Just us two. We'll talk things out."

"There are two things you said, Nick, that I don't like. You said 'you like me.' We had been saying a lot more than that. And if you got something big to say, you can't expect me to wait until Friday."

"Tomorrow then. After school. I promise."

She sighed and I could picture her frown. "Okay. I guess one sleepless night is better than five. My place?"

"Yeah, I'll come over after practice, okay?"

"Okay. And Nick. I do love you."

I felt pretty terrible right about now. The only thing that came to mind was *it's not you; it's me*, but that's a pretty shitty thing to say no matter the situation. I had enough for another lie in me.

"I love you too, Darcie. I do." If you have to add emphasis, you should know it's probably not true.

Chapter Ten

Coach slammed his clipboard on the gym floor and kicked a basketball. "Where is your hustle? What is wrong with you guys?"

Well, it's six in the morning, and your starters were all hung-over yesterday. Yeah, we're not at our best.

I threw two passes that were stolen, couldn't hit a three pointer to save my life, and heaved like a smoker running up and down the court. Jared tried to dunk and missed. Asantà hadn't hit a single shot, and he was a pro at his fade away.

"This is disgusting! Is this what I can expect all season?"

Only if you make us get up this early every day, I wanted to say.

Toby missed his classic sideline three-pointer, a shot he was famous for at Worthless High. No one was guarding him. Coach grabbed his whistle, threw it across the gym, and shouted, "Suicides! All of you! You're killing me. I'm gonna kill you."

We spent the rest of practice running suicide drills up and down the court. Zack and I threw up in the locker room at the end of practice. It was like being hung-over all over again, without the fun of the party.

And to think: we get to do it all over again in a few hours after school. Isn't sport so much fun?

*****

Afternoon practice was no better. We were even more tired. Zack passed to Toby, and an underclassman easily stole it. Jared missed several easy rebounds. I could barely dribble.

"Coach, we're just tired. Cut us some slack. It's the first practice. We'll get it tomorrow," Asantà, our fearless leader, spoke up.

"Let me help you sleep extra well tonight. On the line. More suicides! Let's go!" Coach yelled. All the players gave us nasty looks. After several suicide drills, most of the team joined Zack and I in throwing up once again in the locker room.

Asantà's locker was next to mine. We needed showers, sleep, and food. We both got undressed at the same time, nothing weird for athletes, but I noticed something a little different: he threw his towel around his waist quicker than he had before. Did he not realize I had seen him naked a hundred times? And did he think that just the sight of a dick would turn me into some rapist? I was tired, hungry, and pissed. I followed him into the shower with a chip on my shoulder.

"What's your problem, man? I thought you were cool."

"What are you talking about?"

"I saw how quickly you put that towel on. Like you didn't want me to see you."

"Maybe I don't. What's wrong with that?"

"That's the same as saying 'fuck no' when I asked you if you were gay. You think I'm some sicko or something?"

Asantà looked around, perhaps shocked at my boldness. But like I said, I was tired, I was hungry, and when I feel that way, anything can come out of my mouth.

"Dude. It's the first time I undressed in front of you since you told me. I'm sorry if it's a little weird. I don't mean nothin' by it."

"We're still bros, you and me. I'm not gonna get a boner if I see your junk." My cheeks were red and my heart beat hard. My anger was like an out of body experience. You ever just feel furious and want to yell, even if it's over something small and innocuous? Exhaustion simply ripped through me.

Fortunately, Asantà had some humor left in him. I think sleepy Asantà equaled silly Asantà, and he battled my bitterness with a little humor of his own.

"Oh yeah." He turned and faced me in the shower and grabbed his balls. He pulled up and down. "This do it for you, *bro*. You like what you see. *Oh, Nick. Suck on these cock and balls!"*

I couldn't help but laugh and that egged him on all the more.

"Oh you laughin' at these cock and balls! Let's see how you laugh now, sucka!" He chased me down in the shower. I fell forward and landed on my knees. He grinded his nude self against my rear. "You like that baby? I got lots of this for you!"

We both laughed hard, the argument forgotten, me feeling stupid. We rolled on our backs in the group locker room shower, showing everything nature gave us.

"You guys are a bunch of homos," another player said walking in the shower. "Gross."

Asantà stood up then and walked towards this other guy, letting everything hang loose. "Oh yeah. We're a team, bitch. I'd be happy to be a homo and love my teammates. If you don't love your team, you got no right to be on it."

"Geez, calm it. I'm sorry, man," he said.

"And don't say homo. It's offensive, asshole."

"Okay, sorry. And shit man, my uncle is gay. I'm no homophobe."

"I'm not gay," Asantà said. "But that don't matter. It's the principle. You use words like gay or homo or faggot around here, and you'll get your ass kicked. Understood?"

"Understood." It was awkward to see Asantà and this dude argue. They were both nude, standing in the middle of the showers. And okay, okay, I'll confess something other gay guys won't want me to say. We do check you out. Sure. It's not like we're attracted to all dicks. But c'mon. They're like boobs. If they're out, we take a look. And I swear Asantà's little power charge here made him semi-erect. The other guy: it was like his dick retreated, a turtle hiding in its shell. When it comes to power, size does matter.

Asantà faced me, fully nude. "You still think I gotta problem? How often will I have to prove it?"

"Anytime I need you to, I hope," I said.

He nodded. "Now go shower. You smell like shit."

*****

I may have smelled fresh, but I was tired as hell. Still, there was one more thing I had to do today. It was time to have THE TALK with Darcie. I didn't know if I had the energy, but I promised her I'd come over after school and that's what I was going to do.

But first, I needed some advice. I didn't know who to ask who may have been in this situation before, and then I thought of the only other guy I knew at this school who was kinda like me: Steve. Fortunately, he programmed his number into my phone, and so before going to Darcie's, I gave him a ring.

"HEYLO," Steve answered.

"Hey. It's Nick."

"I know so many Nick's in my life. You'll have to be more specific."

"Nick Revel. We . . . uh . . . talked at the dance."

"I know who you are silly. Just giving you a hard time. What's up?"

"I hope it's okay to call. I feel bad for what I'm going to ask. But you were . . . you know, nice to me at the dance. Thank you for that, by the way."

"Of course. No need to thank me. I guess this isn't a 'will you go out with me' call?"

"Um, no, not exactly. I'm sorry."

88

"No worries, honey. A heart as big of mind can take being broken. What can I do ya for?"

Steve was confident, strong, and honest. I really kinda hated that I didn't like him. He's exactly who I wanted to be in a way.

"I think I'm about to break up with my girlfriend."

"Oh, honey. About time. What do you need? A knife to put through her heart?"

"Funny."

"You can have the one you put in mine."

"Still funny. I'm being serious though. She doesn't know . . . you know . . . "

"That you like cock?"

I choked a bit. "I wasn't going to say it to her like that, but yeah. She doesn't know I like cock."

"You want to know not how to break up with her, but how to come out to her and make yourself not look like an asshole," Steve said. "Am I right?"

"Damn. Yeah, pretty much."

"The hot gay boys never want to look like assholes. Even if they are."

"Hey now," I said. "I'm trying to do the right thing here."

"There's a first for everything," Steve said in his humorous bitchy tone. "Okay, how much time do we have to prepare?"

"I'm on my way to her house now."

"Jesus, Mary, and Homo Joseph! You should have given me more time!"

"I don't have more time, Steve."

"Okay, honey, it's your funeral. I'll help you write the eulogy."

"Did you ever date a girl?"

"Oh sure."

"Really?"

"I was completely in love with a girl. Her name was Katherine. Most beautiful girl in the world," he told me.

"What happened?"

"We graduated kindergarten and she left me for some kid with a Hot Wheels race track."

Laughing, I replied, "I see."

"It's not funny. I was really in love. She had the best hair and the best shoes. I recognized that even as a five-year-old."

"Okay, Steve, so tell me, with your wide experience, how do I break up with Darcie and not be an asshole?"

"You don't."

"Don't break up with her?" I was confused.

"No, you can't try to *not* be an asshole. You are an asshole. That's your best way out of this."

"I don't want to be an asshole."

"You should have thought about that before you went out with a girl. Yeah, you got your own problems and unique reasons for being an asshole, but your best argument is to start with the fact that you are an asshole."

"So I say: I'm an asshole and I'm gay?"

"Kinda. The secret I think is to make it all about you. Don't make it about her. Even if she does have a vagina. You're the asshole who dated it."

"Jesus." I rubbed my forehead. I wasn't sure if Steve was crazy or genius.

"He won't help you here. The worse you make yourself, the better it will be. You have to be the jerk, the asshole, the coward, the guy too scared to tell the truth who was willing to break a girl's heart."

"That's actually kinda true," I told him.

"Of course it is. That's the point."

I grinned. He certainly had a point. "Thanks for the pep talk."

"That's why you called me, bitch. Now go be honest and get on with your life so she can get on with hers. She deserves that, too."

"You're right. I didn't think I'd say this, but thanks, Steve."

"You're welcome, homo. Call me when you need a date and not break up advice, okay?"

"Okay." I laughed.

"You'll never call me, will you?"

"Maybe, you never know."

"I'll take it. Good luck, Nick."

"Thanks, Steve."

*****

Here's what I thought of on my way to Darcie's house. I didn't want to be this guy. For whatever reason, I fell for a guy in minutes and couldn't even talk to him about it. The minutes I spent with Derek were like a distant dream. When I met him, I had to pretend to be asleep to make any kind of move, and it was a lame move. Then the best thing in the world happened: he liked me back! We had an amazing day together, and so many days had passed since then. Don't you think I wonder how awesome my days could have been had I been stronger? I could be spending my time with Derek, laughing and loving and living in the moment, not trying to find ways to avoid going to a girl's DOWN THERE or developing a strategy for THE TALK.

Feeling the way I do is *not* a choice. Acting the way I do *is* a choice. And because of my own cowardice, my fears of being rejected, my terror at how even random strangers may view me, I chose not to stand up for the only person in this world who made me feel truly alive. If you think being gay is a choice, you're a fucking moron. I'd do anything to live like a straight guy. To ask a girl out without worry as to what her sexual orientation was. To hold hands with a girl without having to hide it or worry about strange looks in public. To not having to think about being brave or being a coward but rather just fucking *being*!

Anyone can hold hands with someone of the opposite sex and not get judged! I can't even do that. Don't get me wrong: I didn't say I'd give anything to be straight. I said I'd give anything to live like a straight guy. I don't want to change. I am who I am. Period. Who I am is natural. I know that. We all should know that. But that doesn't make it any less hard to be who we are. What if Derek were a girl and I were a straight guy? This wouldn't be a story, or it would be a very boring story. No, it's not that easy. I had to hide my affection from him, and I lost him because I was scared. I hurt my friends. I'm hurting Darcie and probably my family because I'm not brave enough to speak the truth. When will this change? When will we look back and think about how ridiculous this all was?

"What? You were embarrassed as a teenager to hold a boy's hand on the bus? That's silly. What was wrong with you?"

What an amazing future that would be.

People look at us differently, even if they say they accept us. Acceptance is the rookie on a turbulent road to success. It's going to be a long time before I can hold a boy's hand in any city in Indiana, or any state for that matter, and not get looked at as being different.

It makes me shake with anger and frustration to the point where sometimes I want to cry and give up. Maybe just go back to the pre-puberty kid who didn't have hormones and wanted to collect Ninja Turtles. I could dream of action and adventure and not the happy/sad dreams of love that I may never fucking have. I never believed in love at first sight. But I experienced it. I met a guy and knew he was the one for me. I don't care if you don't think that's possible. It happened. I miss him with every fiber of my being, and it's all my fault.

I don't know what's worse—losing him or knowing it was all fault.

All my fault.

The last part there: That's exactly what I decided to tell Darcie.

*****

"It's all my fault," I told her after she took me up to her bedroom. Her parents were home this time. I hadn't been in her bedroom since homecoming and the frightening DOWN THERE experience.

"I don't understand what happened to us," she told me.

Believe it or not, I missed Jack Daniels right then. Even if I had just recovered from the world's worst hangover.

"You deserve a better answer than I can possibly articulate."

"Try. Please, try." Darcie started to cry. Here's something else I was learning. When you date someone you really aren't in to, you see them differently. You begin to see them as a chore. They take your time and your energy when you could be doing other things, and because of that you view them in negative light. You know how annoyed I was with Darcie. I couldn't stand the constant need for reassurance with every "I love you" or "I miss you." But c'mon—if you were dating me, wouldn't you need that reassurance? I thought of Steve's advice, and I started to recognize that yes, I really was an asshole.

"First, let me say, I will always like you. I know I'm not saying 'love.' I'm sorry for that. But I will always like you."

"You're breaking up with me, aren't you?" A few weeks ago I would have been annoyed or would have even made fun of the fact that she was crying. In this moment right here, I finally saw her as . . . as a real person, I guess, and not someone who had a life mission to nag me. She really did like me or even love me. She wasn't just some needy girl. She was a person. It seemed so common sense, but it didn't make sense until right now.

"I'll let you make that decision. I think you'll be the one who breaks up with me. You deserve the truth. And tonight, that's what I'm giving you. Every ounce of the truth, no matter how much it hurts me. Or hurts you. Because you deserve to know that it's not your fault."

"I don't understand," she said. She was never more beautiful to me than in that moment: a heartbroken girl with no premonition about what I was going to tell her.

"I'm not one to share a lot of details I guess, but let me try. I'm going to tell you a fact. And then I'm going to try to explain." I took a deep breath and tried to think. "Three facts actually. Then let me fully explain, okay?"

"Okay."

"First, you are beautiful and wonderful and nice and the perfect girlfriend. Any guy would be lucky to have you."

"But not you?"

"Let me tell you the other two facts. Second, I'm an asshole. I've lied. I've acted in ways that I thought were in my best interests, not yours. I'm really an asshole." Sighing, I rubbed my forehead. My head felt hot, and my temples pulsed. "I'm so sorry for that. I didn't even know I was an asshole that's how much of an asshole I was. And that leads me to the third and perhaps most important fact that affects our relationship." I paused here. I don't think I had come out to anyone voluntarily, not really. Jen pretty much already knew. Asantà saw me with Steve. I could easily just end my relationship with Darcie by telling her it's not working or whatever. But I needed to be honest. Not only for her, but for me. I hoped that honesty would lead me to a path of strength, something I desperately needed.

"Third . . . you need to know . . . I need to tell you . . ." I stumbled on my words. She looked up at me with hunger in her eyes. Hunger for some truth, some reasoning, some explanation as to why we weren't the couple we could have been.

"Darcie, I'm gay."

Her eyes and mouth widened, but she didn't say a word.

"That's why I've been an asshole. I've been trying to be someone I'm not. That's why, I guess, I can't really love you in the way you want to be loved."

"You're . . . . gay?" she said after a moment.

"I like dick as much as you," I tried to joke.

I thought she was going to cry, but then she laughed. "I honestly thought it was me. It *really* was you. All along." She paused, grabbed a tissue, and wiped the tears from her eyes. "Why did you date me?"

"It's a long story. But I promise I'll tell you as much as you want to know. Just know that I'm sorry. I didn't mean to hurt you. I just wanted to try and be normal. No, I don't like saying that. That means gay isn't normal. This is what I mean by complicated, you see?"

"Yeah. I get it. I do." And she hugged me. Out of all the hugs we had ever shared, this one meant the most. This was the most honest moment we had. And she didn't hate me. She was beginning to understand me.

"Tell me everything," she said.

"Oh boy. Okay. Well . . ." I started from the beginning. From even before meeting Derek. I started with the kinds of things I looked up online. How I always knew but didn't want to know. Then I talked about meeting Derek. How I fell for him in that one day. How I lost him due my stupid fear. I continued and told her what I had told Jen, and everything between Asantà and me. I told her everything.

And you know what she said to me?

"I love you, Nick. As a friend now. But I love you, okay? You will always be my friend."

"I love you, too." It was the first time I said that to her and meant it. Isn't it funny how much we hide from others to belong and to feel loved? But the most love I have ever felt is when I was completely honest, when I was accepted without having to lie.

When someone loves you when you're pretending to be someone else, that's not love. When someone loves you for being real, that's beautiful. Sure, we had broken up, and in doing so it was the first time we really loved each other.

Because it was the first time we really knew each other.

Chapter Eleven

Come late November, we slept, ate, and bled nothing but basketball. We managed to bounce back from our pitiful practices that first week to become the team we always wanted to be. As lead point guard, my eye had sharpened and my passing and assists led us to victory. Three games in, and I had the most assists on the team. Zack, our other guard, nailed three-pointers as easily as you might wad up a piece of paper and toss it into a garbage can. He led the team in the threes and Toby as forward had the most jump shots on our team. Jared, our giant center, led the entire district in rebounds, and Asantà led the district in most points scored. Asantà and I were an unbeatable pair. He'd cut across that court, and I could pass to him without even looking. He'd drive it down the lane for an easy lay-up. Out of three games, we had three wins. The school was starting to get behind us, and our coach, the angry monster, actually smiled once in a while. We were the team to beat, and we had an impeccable, diverse set of starters who complemented one another's skills.

Life after the Halloween party had been all basketball. Darcie came to the games, cheered us on, and went out to dinner with us afterwards. The guys knew we had broken up and were only friends. I could tell Jared, Toby, and Zack thought it was a little strange that she still hung around with us, but they were too excited about our victories to question it.

"Hey, Asantà," I had said before our first game. I told him about Darcie and me. "I will tell the guys and the rest of the team. But let's not do anything to distract from the season. When we get into our groove and the timing feels right, I'll tell them, okay?"

He may have become my number one supporter, but nothing stood between him and basketball. "Cool. Yeah. Minds on the game. We need to stay focused."

I was curious if he had feelings for Darcie and if he would act out on those feelings now that we were broken up, but true to his word, he kept his mind on the game. That didn't stop a little flirting here and there when we all went out, but so far nothing had come of it.

After our third game and victory, we went out to our local Steak 'n Shake to grab burgers and of course their delicious milk shakes. Steak 'n Shake was our go-to place to hang out.

"Good game tonight, guys. Good game!" Asantà said. "I've got a good feeling that we're going to state, and we're gonna win. That'll show all those football dudes."

The football team made it to the playoffs and went pretty far, but they lost and didn't make it all the way to state. It's terrible to take joy in another's misery, I know, but we were happy. You have to understand. When one sport dominates a school for decades, it's like all the others don't even matter. We told ourselves we weren't doing this just for us or for basketball, but for all the sports, for all the athletes who work their asses off every day but don't get the recognition because they don't play under Friday night lights in the big stadium.

"To state!" Toby cheered.

"It's a few months off, but if we keep our heads in the game like we've been doing, we got a good chance," Asantà said. "A great chance."

"Hell, yeah," I added.

"You guys are great out there," Darcie said. "Seriously. You're all so fast. It's much more fun to watch than football too. Much more action, very quick up and down the court. Football is so boring," she told us.

We laughed, even if she was exaggerating to make us feel good. It worked.

"You guys gotta try this banana and chocolate side-by-side." Zack took a big drink of his shake. "This is heaven."

"Let me try," Jared said and in one big gulp he swallowed the rest of Zack's shake.

"Hey, you owe me a new one!" We all laughed.

"This is nice," Toby said. "I never want it to end."

He didn't need to explain. We understood. Youth and sports and late nights out and endless milkshakes: not everything lasts forever.

"Can I have your cherry?" Asantà asked Darcie.

"Dude, don't be crude," Jared said.

"Yeah, man. That's nasty," Toby agreed.

"I'm talking about the cherry in her shake, pervs," Asantà said.

"We know what you're talking about." Zack laughed. "I thought Nick took that cherry."

"Boys, you're in the presence of a lady, and that talk is not appropriate," Darcie joked.

"A lady? Where?" I looked around and she slapped me jokingly.

"So, whatever happened between you guys?" Jared asked. There it was. Sooner or later, someone had to ask it.

"We learned that we're better as friends. That's all," Darcie answered for us. "Sometimes you date for a while, and you realize that you're not best as a couple. So you decide: do we remain friends or do we go our separate directions? Nick is my best friend now."

"He's *my* best friend," Asantà said.

"Nick is everyone's best friend," Zack joined in. "That's why we love him."

"Aww, guys, you're making me blush."

They laughed and Toby threw whip cream at Zack, who grabbed the ketchup bottle and was about to shoot ketchup back at him when the server came to the table.

She coughed to get our attention. "Will there be anything else? Besides the mess you all are going to clean up before you leave?"

"Sorry, miss," Jared said. "We'll leave a nice tip."

"You better," she said.

We all left a few bucks, not bad for a group of teenagers. "What now?" Darcie asked as we left.

"Yeah, what now?" I turned and looked at Asantà.

"Let's crank the stereo and drive all night."

If you're old, that probably sounds like a waste of time and gas. If you're young, it sounds like the perfect way to spend one's night.

Toby had borrowed his mom's van for the night so we could all ride together. He drove, Jared took shotgun, and the rest of us sat in the back. We cranked the stereo, hit the highway, drove as fast as Toby was willing, and sang along to random songs until we had no voice left.

It was a perfect night.

*****

Our fourth game took us on the road. Extra nervousness pulsated throughout my arms and legs, making them shake and bounce during the entire bus ride there, but not for any ordinary reason. We were playing the Mayville High Tornadoes. Don't think I haven't forgotten that the one time I saw Derek after our trip was when our football team played Mayville. Maybe it was only my imagination, but I still swear he was in the stands that night at our football stadium.

When we arrived to play, I scanned the gymnasium for any sign of him. Of course, nothing ever seemed to go my way when searching for him, and there was no sign of him in the gym. We stood for the national anthem. I mouthed the words while my eyes were busy scanning every face in the crowd. But no, nothing.

The announcer did our starting line-up and we roared and cheered, trying to pump adrenaline into our systems. It was our first away game, and we actually had a bus full of students and community supporters come with us. It wasn't a huge turnout, but it was the biggest turnout we ever had on an away game, at least in my experience as a Worthless High Wasp.

We listened to the starting line-up of the other team. Their supporting section was full, on their feet, and screaming. We were a little envious, but we were also determined to shut them up. That was one of the best feelings and challenges when playing basketball: to shut up the rival team's supporters.

The announcer was on the last member of the Tornado's starting lineup. "And at guard . . . five foot eleven . . . number thirty-three . . . Derek Burka!"

It was moments before the game started, and I about had a heart attack on the gym floor. Running through and high-fiving several teammates, there he was, sporting a basketball jersey and the number thirty-three. The guy I had been hoping to find for months. There was Derek.

My Derek.

Months of searching, months of hoping, months of endless optimism, and months of moments where I told myself to give up and BOOM, like a sporadic firecracker exploding in November for no reason, THERE HE WAS.

On the basketball court.

Against me. In the same damn position as me.

Oh, Jesus. I'd have to guard him and he'd have to guard me during the game. Oh, fuck. A swarm of killer butterflies attacked my stomach, and I swallowed forcefully multiple times hoping I wouldn't throw up.

"Dude, you okay?" Asantà asked.

"Uh, uh, it's . . . um." I couldn't even find the words to say.

The Tornados huddled and Asantà pulled us together. "Get it together, Nick. Okay, guys, you ready. This will be our fourth win tonight and our first on the road. We need this. Wasps on three."

"WASPS!" everyone shouted but me. It was like I was having an out of body experience. I was moving, but I didn't feel like I was in control of who I was.

Did Derek see me? Did he know it was me out here?

Jared and the other team's center faced off for first possession. Jared tipped the ball towards me, but Derek jumped out in front of me and grabbed it. He dribbled and motioned for his team to organize.

I had a flashback to the day he won me the stuffed lion at Kings Island. It was a basketball game. He easily made the shot, even on the offset carnival rim meant to screw you. All this time, he was a basketball player, a guard, just like me.

For the first time since the game began, Derek made eye contact. His eyes grew and his mouth dropped. This was as much of a surprise to him as it was to me.

"Nick?" he said.

My mouth moved, I think, but I have no idea if any words came out.

We must have looked ridiculous. We were the only two on the other side of the court. The rest of our teammates had already gathered on the Tornado's side to play the first possession.

I saw surprise and shock. But I didn't see hate. That was something.

"Hey!" one of Derek's teammates called out.

He snapped back to reality, and his shock turned into determination.

"We got a game to play," he said, and he dribbled right past me.

His team was fast. He passed to the forward who dodged Toby and took it straight to the rim.

Asantà took the ball out and passed it in to me. He ran passed and gave me a look. "Head in the game, Nick!"

It was my turn to face Derek. As I passed the half court line, he got right up in my face. I looked him in those eyes, those dark, beautiful eyes, and then he stole the ball right out from under me, ran to the other side of the court, and made an easy layup.

"Dude." Zack confronted me. "Get with it."

Once again Asantà passed the ball to me to take down the court. Once again, he gave me a nasty look.

I can't look at him. That's the only way to win. I can't think about him. I passed quickly to Zack, who passed to Toby, who shot a nice fade away and scored our first two points.

My strategy was working. I avoided all eye contact with Derek, as much as I wanted to look at him. It was harder when I was guarding him. I reached out for steal and got caught fouling him, but touching him would be worth a dozen fouls.

I allowed myself to watch him as he took the free throw line. He had great arms, thick biceps, well-defined triceps shaped like diamonds. The broad, strong shoulders and the thick chest that breathed heavily in and out took me back to that day I had met him. And I had to confess: the basketball shorts were nice on him, too. He had athletic, smooth legs, and shiny, fine hair. I felt like I had an apple caught in my throat. I could barely breathe. As he made both free-throws, I had to pull myself back in the game. We were losing.

Asantà passed to me, and I dribbled hard down the court. Toby set up a screen, I drove past, and Asantà cut down center. Without looking, I tossed the ball directly to him, and he cut under the basket for an underhand layup. He high-fived me. "That's my boy!"

On the other side of the court, Derek faked a pass and I went for it. He then set up for a three-pointer and nailed it.

Both teams played hard and firm. We were pretty evenly matched, but at half-time, the Tornados led the Wasps 42-35.

*****

As the team ran into the locker room for half-time, Asantà grabbed me and pulled me behind. "Dude, what's going on with you? We should be beating this team, but you're distracted."

"Do you remember when you asked if there was a guy I liked and I said yes but you didn't know him?"

"Yeah."

"It's the guy I'm guarding."

"What?"

"It's a long story. I met him last summer. I didn't know he even went to this school. I had no idea he'd be on this team. I haven't talked to him since last summer. It ended bad. It was my fault."

He shook his head. "Why am I not surprised?"

"I know, I know."

"Should we get you out of this game?"

"No, I'm okay. I promise. It was just a complete shock. We'll get them in the second half."

"We better," he said and joined the rest of the team in the locker room.

*****

We started off strong in the second half. I refused to look Derek in the eye, but he did steal the ball from me once when I looked a little too far below his eyes. Let's just say you could see something swinging in those shorts.

Jared was the one who got our crowd, small but faithful, up on their feet cheering. We spread their defense wide, and I shot a pass straight down the middle to him. He turned and slammed the ball, and our section roared.

In the final minutes of the fourth quarter, our teams were neck and neck. It was 75-73 Tornados, and we had possession. I had the ball at the top and drove down center. Zack looped behind me, and I tossed the ball back. He hit a perfect three, 76-75, Wasps!

Derek took the ball down his side and called out a play to his team. One of his teammates set up a pick on me, and he set up for a perfect three, but out of nowhere, Asantà flew forward and blocked his shot. I ran for the loose ball and drove down the court. I passed it to Asantà on the opposite side, and he made another layup, 78-75, Wasps!

The Tornados called a timeout. We huddled around our coach who said, "We've got a minute left. Don't let them get a three. They can take any other shot, and then you get that ball and you kill the minute. Don't take a shot till the clock is almost out, got it? Wasps on three!"

Derek received the incoming pass from his team, and I guarded him as closely as I could. I tried to keep my mind focused, but I won't lie: It was an adrenaline rush to be that close to him. He passed the ball and ran towards the baseline. I followed him, and as a player passed the ball back to him, he set up for a three. I leapt with all my might to block the shot, and then my hand collided with his arm. He missed, but I got called on another foul. This would give Derek three free-throws.

We lined up, Asantà swatted me on the ass, and said, "It's okay. Good effort."

Derek positioned himself at the free-throw line and sunk three perfect shots. The game was tied up.

Our coach called a time-out with forty-five seconds left on the clock.

"Our strategy is the same, but we have to make the shot now or go into overtime. We cannot let them get position. Here's our play. He wrote on his white clipboard and set it up for Zack to pick Derek and Asantà to cut from one side to the other. I'd pass to Toby, who'd pass to Asantà, who was to drive in for a layup.

"Wasps on three!"

Zack tossed the ball into me. First, we had to run the clock down. I threw to Toby, who passed to Zack, who threw it back to me. Fifteen seconds left. It was time for the play. Zack set up the pick, and I went to pass to Toby, but Derek saw it coming. He rolled around the pick and intercepted the pass. Ten seconds left. He ran with the ball down the court, and with only a few seconds remaining made a layup. The Tornados' cheering section was up on their feet, screaming at the top of their lungs. Our section had been shut up. It was 80-78, Tornado victory. We had our first defeat of the season, and like everything bad that happens, I once again thought it was all my fault.

Chapter Twelve

At the end of the game, the teams formed two rows and high-fived each other. "Good game, good game, good game," we all said to be sportsmanlike. As Derek approached me for our high-five and "good game," I wanted to grab him and talk to him. But there was no time. He made eye contact and nodded, but it was only a high-five and then both teams retreated into separate locker rooms.

Coach slammed his fist into a locker. "We got out hustled! That's it. We have much more talent than they do. You let them out hustle you, and that's exactly how we lose our chances at a state championship!" This was the time when I hated sports. We worked our asses off, we a bunch of sweaty and tired teens. And now we had to be lectured on not being good enough. If I didn't love the game, this would be the shit that would make me quit.

We were to shower and be on the bus in twenty minutes. I took the quickest shower of my life. I was not missing an opportunity to catch Derek. I cleaned up and got dressed and ran to the other team's locker room. It certainly would be unethical to enter, if not dangerous. An opposing team does not enter the other's locker room. So I waited outside and kept checking my phone. I had ten minutes before I was supposed to be back on our bus. C'mon, someone leave that damn locker room.

A prayer had actually been answered. It wasn't Derek, but it was one of their players. "Hey, man," I said. "Good game, again. Um, I was wondering if you could get Derek for me. Can you tell him someone wants to talk to him out here?"

"Okay, I guess. Who are you?"

"Just tell him it's a friend. Please." He would know it was me, I'm sure, but I thought if the request was ambiguous he'd at least come check it out and not ignore me.

"Okay."

I looked at my phone again. Seven damn minutes. I have seven minutes to make a difference. I sighed hard, leaned against the wall, my foot bouncing impatiently.

And then he appeared. He had showered, his hair was down, straight, and smooth. I think I liked it even better like that. He wore a tight, white undershirt and jeans, no shoes or shocks.

"Hey," he greeted. Okay, at least he's speaking to me.

"Hey," I said. I struggled to think of what to say while my heart pounded hard enough to make my chest explode. "Good game."

"Thanks. You, too."

"So, uh, this is weird, huh?" *C'mon, Nick, you can do better that that!* "I never expected to run into you like this."

"Yeah. Me neither. I had no idea you played basketball." He looked down at the floor. I just wanted him to look me in the eyes and smile and tell me that he also had been thinking of me every damn second of every damn day.

"I didn't know you did either." I swallowed hard, trying to think. Another minute must have passed, and I had nothing to show for it.

We stood in silence for a moment, and I could picture the team getting on the bus, coach doing a head count, looking around, and getting pissed that I wasn't there.

"I've wanted to talk to you for a long time." My eyes stung with tears. *Don't you dare let them out.*

"Okay," was his only response. I wish he'd smile or something. *Don't you know you're like all I think about?* How could he not have more of a reaction?

"I've been looking for you for a long time."

"Yeah?" He looked up then. His eyes were sad, but not angry.

"Yeah. Not to sound creepy but I tried searching for you online, on social media. Never found anything."

"I'm not online. I know. People give me shit for it all the time. From what I know, it all seems like a time-killer. And people are too fake online. I'd rather not be a part of that, you know?"

"That's cool," I said.

More silence. I could imagine coach cussing right about now. I was cussing at myself. *How do I tell him how I feel?*

"And if you tried to Google anything about our team, some crazy mom got the school to stop putting our names on the website." He rolled his eyes. "Some helicopter mom who said creeps could be trying to stalk the kids." He looked at me closely. "Maybe she was right."

I wanted to laugh, but I couldn't. After a moment of silence, I said, "I'm supposed to be getting back on the bus."

"Okay." So taciturn. Was this the same Derek I had met last summer? Or was this the Derek I had hurt?

"Okay, I'm just going to say it." I took a deep breath and thought, *well, fuck it. What have I got to lose?* "I was a complete idiot that night. Not a single damn day goes by that I don't wish I could turn back time. I'd leave that hotel room and sleep in the hall or outside if I meant I was able to hang with you longer. I was such an idiot. But I also want you to know that the day we had together . . . that was honestly the best day I've ever had in my entire life. I can't stop thinking about it. And to find you, here, like this. That means something, don't you think?"

He didn't say anything but he smiled ever so slightly. It was like he wanted to smile, but he was being careful, guarded.

"Can you ever forgive me?" I asked.

"Nick," he started. "It took me a long time to be comfortable being me. I promised myself I wouldn't waste any time on anyone who was scared, who wouldn't stand up for themselves. Who wouldn't stand up for me. Even if I did really like the person."

"You really liked me?" I asked.

"Yeah, I did." He smiled and I wanted to touch him again, more than anything.

"Will you forgive me?" The damn tears stung my eyes, and I reached out and grabbed his hand.

"Yeah, I will." He squeezed back.

"Will you give me a second chance to get to know you? For you to get to know me?"

Before he could answer, Asantà ran across the gym and hollered. "Nick! Coach is pissed. You need to get back here." Then Asantà looked at who I was talking to. He slowed to a jog and approached.

"Hey. I'm Nick's best friend, Asantà."

Derek let go of my hand. "I'm Derek."

"You really messed up my friend, you know that? Like he's been one hot mess all year."

"Really?" Derek raised his eyebrows as if checking me out.

"Yeah. And I don't know if I like that. But if he likes you, you'd be stupid to turn him away. He's the best friend I could have." Then Asantà turned to me. "I'll tell coach you've got the shits and get you a few extra minutes."

"Gee, thanks." I laughed. Asantà turned and ran back to the locker room. "So, hey." I turned back to Derek.

"Hey."

"What do you think?" I asked him.

"I think you've got a pretty cool friend." Derek smiled.

"Yeah."

"You were really messed up? After that day?" He frowned a bit, and his eyes . . . it was as if they could look into my soul.

"I can't get you out of my head." I paused, blinked, and swallowed hard. "You have no idea. I've been . . ." *Crying myself to sleep? Listening to super sad music? Kissing a boy in the bathroom at a school dance? Picturing you when I'm in the shower and . . .*

Clearing my throat, I continue. "Derek, yes. Not a single day has passed that you haven't been on my mind. I look for you wherever I go, always praying I'd run into you someday. And now, here you are. And I don't want to leave. Never again."

"And you've . . . you've told your friends about it, too?"

"Not all. But yeah, some. I've started. I've changed a lot. Because . . . because of you." My arms shook. My stomach danced, making my insides feel so funny. "This has to mean something, seeing you here, right? Go out with me. Give me another chance. I promise I won't screw it up."

Derek took out his phone. "What's your number?" He smiled.

I nearly shouted the numbers, like I had won the lottery, and he entered them in his phone. Then he started texted something. My phone went off and I read the text. It read, 'Yes.'

"Yes?" I almost jumped.

"Yes. Let's get to know each other. And now you have my number."

I wanted to hug him, to kiss him, to grab him, something, anything physical. But I forced myself to take a deep breath.

We were going to get to know each other. This wasn't a marriage proposal or something crazy like that. This was the end of a terrible mystery and the beginning of a new adventure.

"You shouldn't keep your team waiting too long." He smiled, now bigger, the bright and beautiful smile I remembered.

"If only they knew how long I've waited." No, I was not going to be the first one to leave. The team would have to come in with shotguns to get me to leave right now.

"When are you free?" He was so damn cute. On the outside, he may have been ripped and hot. But in this moment, I saw the teenage boy inside of him, too. The shy, curious boy who was as excited as me.

"I could be free any time," I told him.

"Tomorrow, then. Let's hang out. Call me when you get home tonight, and we'll figure something out."

"Okay," I stood there just beaming as if living a great dream and never wanting to wake up, not willing or perhaps even capable of leaving.

And then he surprised me again. He stepped in close, put a hand on the back of my head, and pulled me closer. We were face to face, noses almost touching. He held me there, looked into my eyes, and I swear time and motion and life completely stopped. We were locked in this position, and I never wanted it to end. He leaned in even closer. I could feel his breath on my face as he whispered, "I've thought about you too these last few months. I was mad that next morning, you know, but I'd be lying if I didn't tell you how much I regretted throwing away your name and number."

"Up until that, it was the best day I have ever had," I whispered back, our lips almost touching.

He smiled, then he closed his eyes, pushed his face forward, eliminating that inch gap between our lips, and he kissed me.

It was like every system in my body shut down and fully awoke all at once. I kissed him back, gently but passionately.

After a few moments, which felt absolutely perfect yet not long enough, he pulled away. We didn't need words. Our bodies had said it all.

He released me, his arms falling away slowly, like gentle snowflakes lingering in the air, and went back into the locker room. I pretty much skipped back to the bus.

It was the new best day of my life.

Chapter Thirteen

Dinner first, no movie: that's what we had decided on for our first date night. We wanted time to talk, to hang, to really get to know each other. It was getting really cold in central Indiana, but early December hadn't brought any snow yet. Mayville was about twenty minutes from Worthlapp, but there was a laser tag place close to Mayville, and we thought that would be a fun after dinner activity. So I met Derek in his hometown.

My to-do list grew, and time was of the essence, as they say. I couldn't be going out on dates with a guy and not tell people, could I? I still had my parents and my teammates to tell. High school can be a rumor mill as we all know, and even if the rumor was true, I'd rather it come directly from me than from some gossipy kid. I promised myself I'd tell everyone soon. Maybe even this coming week. But there was no time today, and I didn't have the energy anyway. I had to get ready for my first real date with Derek.

I felt stupid staring in my closet trying to think of what to wear. I wanted to look nice of course, and I realized I had never really taken the time to think like this about clothes when I was dating Darcie. I settled on my favorite jeans and a dark but thin sweater that zipped up in the front. I must have spent an hour in the shower, cleaning and scrubbing and wanting to smell perfect. There wasn't much I could do with this short hair, but I tried to make sure it looked perfect. Then I doused myself in probably too much cologne.

I went downstairs, and Mom and Dad were both getting dinner ready in the kitchen.

"Who did you say you were going out with tonight?" Mom asked. I wasn't going to completely lie, in case I might get caught. You never know if one of the guys might show up or something.

So I said, "It's a friend I met playing basketball. We're gonna play laser tag. Over by Mayville."

"You look pretty nice for laser tag," Mom said. "Is this friend a girl?"

"No." I laughed. "Just a guy friend. What's wrong with looking nice?"

Jen giggled in the corner. "Nothing," Mom said. "I'm only curious. Your curfew is midnight."

"I haven't forgotten."

"You smell," Jen told me.

"Thanks."

"Who *is* it?" she whispered.

"Shh. I'll tell ya later." I ran my hand through her hair on the way out. Her excited giggles followed me until I shut the front door.

I got in my car, took a look in the rearview mirror, and texted Derek. *On my way.*

*****

It goes without saying that Derek is hot. I think you must already know that. When I pulled up at his house tonight, he walked out wearing tight, but not too tight, jeans, and a white button up shirt that totally revealed the muscles in his chest and arms. He held on to a brown coat but wasn't wearing it yet.

"Hi," he said, getting into the car.

"Hey." Yeah, my teenage hormones rumbled, and I wanted to skip the date and start making out right there. Instead, I sucked in some air to calm down and asked, "So where to?"

"You like Italian?" *I like you.*

"Yeah." *Steady, now,* I told myself.

"Cool. We have a great Italian place not too far. I'll direct ya."

"Okay."

"Thanks for picking me up."

"No prob." I smiled

I backed out of the driveway, he told me where to go, and then he put his hand on my knee.

Lightning shot up my thigh, and butterflies waged war in my belly. "Remember this?" he asked.

Swallowing a lump in my throat and resisting the urge to pull over and kiss him, I managed to say, "I'll never forget."

"I got the biggest kick out of you trying to touch me on that bus when we met. You pretended to be asleep, didn't you? Just to feel me up. Such a perv." He laughed.

I nodded. "I am pretty lame."

"No, I'm only joking. It was . . . cool. For someone to want to touch me like that." He squeezed my leg, and I reached down to hold his hand. "And so you know, the feeling was and is mutual."

My heart was beating really fast, and it felt like was back on those roller coaster rides from when I first met him. It was already turning out to be a perfect evening.

*****

Dinner was great, too. The best thing about Derek is that we never felt like we had to keep talking, and yet there were no awkward silences. Silence comes and goes in conversation, and it felt natural when there was a quiet moment. Derek Burka was a junior in high school like me. He had turned seventeen last month, so he was a few months older. My birthday wasn't until February. He loved basketball and had played all his life. He liked horror movies and all kinds of comedies. We had a mutual love for comedies like *Booksmart, Easy A*, and of course *Love, Simon*.

"The book is better," he said, in regards to *Love, Simon*.

"I haven't read it. The last book I read was *They Both Die in the End.* Have you read that?" I asked.

He shook his head. "Sounds depressing."

"It is, but it's also really, like, inspiring. It's about two boys who both are going to die on the same day and become friends to make the most of the hours they have left."

I liked that he was a reader, too. I had always loved books, but I never had friends who loved to read as much as I did.

I learned that he was an only child, and his parents were divorced.

"It's a really sad story," he said. "I'll tell you. But not tonight. Let's talk about happy things tonight."

He told me he came out about his sexuality the summer before his sophomore year. "But that's part of the same sad story, so I'll tell you about that later, too. It wasn't the easiest experience, but I promised I'd always be honest, and I would make friends with those who were honest." I could tell from the look on his face that he may be alluding to me when I roomed with a bunch of d-bags the night at Kings Island, but he didn't say anything else on the subject.

"So does like your whole school know?"

"Yeah. And believe me, I was worried about hate and bullying. I spent every afternoon my sophomore year in the weight room to bulk up. I figured if I had some muscle on these bones that most jerks would leave me alone." I caught myself staring again at those arms.

"Have they?" I asked.

"Yeah. It's pretty cool actually. There are always cliques and groups that make jokes behind your back. They're easy to spot. But they're the fake people I wouldn't want to be friends with anyway, so I avoid them." He shrugged. His confidence made him even more attractive.

"Wow. Are there other out kids at your school?"

"A few, yeah. A couple guys and a few girls. What about your school?"

I told him about Steve, and I was completely honest about myself. I had only told Asantà, Darcie, and my sister. But I promised him that would all change very soon.

"Have you ever had a boyfriend?" I asked.

"One of the guys asked me out before, and I said yes. But we didn't have anything in common. There wasn't any real . . . spark. You know, no magic knee grabbing." He laughed. "How about you?"

"No. Just a girlfriend." I told him about Darcie and how I came out to her.

He nodded as I told the story. I was worried he'd criticize me for lying to Darcie, for trying to be someone I wasn't, but he just listened. The more I looked at him, the more I realized that he was so strong and brave. I felt like I had a lot of catching up to do.

We kept sharing random interests. He liked to play poker, and I loved the movie *Rounders*. He wanted to major in public relations in college, and I had no idea what I wanted to do with my life. He had the same best friend since grade school. "I'm her GBF. Gay best friend. She's one sarcastic but funny girl. You'll like her."

He was already planning on introducing me to his best friend. That was a certainly a plus.

We finished our dinners, and he insisted on picking up the bill. "You drove this far to get me. Let me pay for dinner."

"Okay, but then I'm paying for laser tag."

"In more than one way, cuz I'm gonna kick your ass." He grinned.

As we got ready to leave, a group of guys and girls in the corner started laughing and looking at us. Did they know we were on a date? How could they know? It was my first time being pointed at and ridiculed like that. Like a bee sting to the ego, I felt my insides swell.

"Ignore them," Derek said. "They're a bunch of douche bags from Burlington. The guys are on their basketball team, actually. They're in our district. You must have played them. And they know about me. They've said some nasty things on the court."

"Oh," I said and looked over at them. One of the guys gestured crudely by pretending to suck a dick, sticking his tongue in his cheek and moving his hand up and down by his mouth. "What a jerk."

"There will always be jerks, Nick. You get tough skin and don't listen to them. And if they do get in your face, you knock their teeth out," he said with a smile, and I wasn't sure if he was joking or not. "They lost to us already this season. Have you played Burlington?"

"Not yet. Now I can't wait to destroy them."

Derek laughed. "Yeah, kick their ass on the court. That's the best way to get back at 'em."

I looked over my shoulder again on the way out, and they continued mocking us. I was having such a great moment, a really fantastic date. It pissed me off that people were like that. That they could take someone else's happiness and try to ruin it by being ignorant, immature assholes.

I did as Derek wanted, though. I ignored them and kept my mouth shut, and let's be honest—I wasn't sure I had what it would take to confront them and say something anyway, but I also reached for and held his hand on the way out. Let that be my "fuck you" to the ignorant, and my wish that Derek will think I'm as strong as I hope to become.

*****

"I feel like a ghostbuster," I said, strapping a laser tag vest on my back and chest. "This is awesome."

"I was hoping you'd like it," Derek said.

"I think we're the oldest ones here."

"It's okay. It's fun to shoot kids." He smirked.

We were strapped up and ready to play, waiting in line for our first game to begin. There was a long line of nearly twenty participants, and we were divided into two teams. Derek and I were on the red team, and we were supposed to shoot as many on the green team as we could. A timer counted down, three, two, one, and we walked briskly into the laser tag arena (we were told not to run, unfortunately, but that was a rule I was hoping we could break under the dark umbrella of the arena).

It was a huge warehouse-style room that had been converted into a laser tag adventure. Props of fake hills, bunkers, and tunnels were set up all around. Fog machines, lasers, and strobe lights made the room a like a sci-fi film, and music pulsated through many large speakers. It was incredible.

"Over there." Derek pointed, and we ran up some stairs. "A higher level is better. We'll get a clear shot of those on the ground." He hid behind a thick cardboard wall and shot down at some kids below. Our laser gun showed how many hits we had accumulated. I already had five, but Derek had eleven.

"Nice shot," I told him.

"Thanks."

We held our ground, but in a few moments some kids snuck up behind us and started shooting.

"Ahhhh!" I screamed and ran towards them, but my gun wouldn't work. Once you've been shot, it was put on a short delay. "Damn kids!"

Derek laughed. "You sound like an old man."

"We'll see who's old. Forget hiding. Let's take them head on." I sprinted like a soldier on a killing spree and Derek followed. We shot everyone in sight. It was hard to tell who was on your team, but you only got points for shooting your opponents. A small green light flashed on the vest and gun of the opposing team, so we looked specifically for those but shot anyone in sight. We ran a full loop upstairs, and then went back down. The majority of the kids were fighting below.

"Okay, let's run and shoot from here to that wall over there. It looks like we can hide behind it," I stated, as if I were a military expert.

"You got it," Derek replied.

"Ahhh!" I yelped and ran again, probably not the best idea, as it gave me away, but I was having too much fun to care. I shot a dozen kids on the ground floor and slid like a baseball player behind the wall. Derek was right behind me.

"I'm up to 20 hits!" I cheered looking at my counter.

"Nice. I'm at 19. You're a natural at shooting small children," he joked.

I laughed. "I'm glad you suggested this. It's awesome."

We hid behind the wall for a moment and then Derek pointed at a tunnel to our right.

"Look," he suggested. "I bet we can hide in there like snipers."

"I'm already sweating from that run," I panted. "Sounds like a good plan to me."

We squeezed into a tunnel, another thick cardboard prop for the room, big enough for two people. We rolled around and faced the ground floor's main fighting area and aimed, ready to attack.

A few kids ran from one hiding space to another. We shot them all. "I'm at 25!" I yelled.

We were shoulder to shoulder in the tunnel. Derek laughed at my enthusiasm. Physically, this was the closest we had probably been all night, and I certainly didn't mind.

"There!" he shouted. Another group of kids. We hit every single one of them and giggled as they whined about the delay they now had on their guns.

"We should do this every weekend!" I looked over at him then and soaked up that smile that won me over many months ago. My heart was beating fast from running and from the adrenaline of the game and the loud, vibrating music. But if it were possible, it beat even harder in this moment.

I was staring too long, I know. I was smiling too big, yes, I know that, too. I was next to the most beautiful, nicest, kindest, strongest person I had ever met. I couldn't help but do what I did next. I moved in as close as possible and kissed him as passionately as I had run across the laser tag arena. He kissed back with equal enthusiasm. I dropped my gun on the tunnel floor and put my arms around him and held him as tightly and closely as possible. This second kiss, somehow, was even better than the first.

"You guys!" a kid yelled behind us and started to giggle. He must have been about ten years old. We didn't realize the tunnel had a back entrance, and unfortunately, he was on the other team. He shot us both, laughed, and ran away.

"Well, ain't that something?" Derek said.

"Huh?"

"You'd think he'd go 'eww' or something. But he only laughed."

I had to think about that for a moment, but then it dawned on me that Derek had observed something great. "You're right. An innocent laugh is much better than an ignorant insult."

"The world is changing. It's a great time to be us."

"Yes, it is definitely a great time," I agreed and kissed him again. His mouth felt perfect against mine, his lips wet, his passion deep, and his smell sweet.

"One minute left!" an announcement called throughout the loud speakers. I could always kiss him longer, but I wanted him to have the most of everything from this night, I thought.

So I said, "Let's charge them all and get as many as we can!"

He nodded, we crawled out of the tunnel, and then we charged at all the kids on the ground floor attacking them as if our lives depended on it. When final results were posted, neither Derek nor I had the most hits. In fact, we weren't even in the top ten. As I leaned on him and laughed and he leaned on me and laughed back, neither of us cared that we hadn't won.

We played two more rounds, but got worse with every round. Of course, we also spent more time in that tunnel every time we played. Neither of us complained.

*****

I dropped him off at his house after that, and like the gentleman I was trying to become, I walked him to his door. Without a word, he pulled me into his arms and kissed me again. Somewhere in the back of my mind, I worried that the neighbors could see, that his mom would see, that someone would insult us. But no one did, and these thoughts didn't appear to be on Derek's mind.

"I had a great night," he said.

"I had a better night," I told him.

"I'm glad we did this."

"Not as glad as me."

"Is that the game we're playing?"

"Only if we can play it again and again," I said.

His lips stretched from ear to ear. "What do you think was better?" he asked. "Tonight or the first day we met?"

"Oh man, that's tough." I had to think for a moment. "Tonight," I decided.

"Why?"

"Because the first day I met you was a dream, a fantasy. Tonight the dream came true."

He kissed me again after that. "What do we do now?" he asked after coming up for air. It was nice to see that there was innocence and wonder behind all of his strength.

"We do this as often as possible. If that's okay with you?" I realized how vulnerable I was in the moment, too, and how important it was to reveal one's vulnerability to those you cared the most about.

"Absolutely," he said.

"Can I call you tomorrow?" I asked. It dawned on me that before I had always been told to call. This was the first time I had asked.

"Of course."

"Okay. Good night, Derek," I said and kissed him one more time.

"Good night, Nick. Drive safe. Text me when you get home. If that's okay." I heard vulnerability in his voice too, and I smiled gently.

"I will. I most definitely will."

On the twenty minute drive home, I played only the happiest of songs off my phone. I sang along the entire time.

Have you had nights like this? The nights when you sing as loud as you can and don't care who hears you are the nights worth remembering for all of time.

Chapter Fourteen

You couldn't wipe the smile from my face if you tried. It was Sunday morning, the day after my date with Derek. I threw on a T-shirt and some sweatpants and went down to join my family for breakfast.

"I smell bacon!" I said.

"Bacon, eggs, hash browns, toast, and juice!" Jen said.

Mom and Dad were working together over the stove. I loved my parents for that. It was never only one or the other who cooked or cleaned; they did everything together.

"My main man, Nick," Dad said. "What will it be this morning?"

"Everything!" I felt like a kid on Christmas morning.

"Then everything it shall be!"

I kept looking at my phone. Derek and I texted each other late into the night. I had fallen asleep and hadn't seen his last text until this morning. Still trying to piece all the texts together in my end-of-night euphoria and fatigue, he had texted, *the fat lady is singing.*

I texted back this morning and wrote, *I'm not a lady. And I'm not fat. But I sang all the way home.* I hadn't heard back from him yet. He was probably still sleeping.

"I know that smile!" Mom said. "You don't look at your phone and smile like that unless it's from someone you really like or it's a funny cat video. So, which is it?"

I looked over at Jen, and she nodded at me with a great big smile of her own. I always had an excuse for not doing what I didn't really want to do. Don't get me wrong. I know I needed to tell my parents, but that doesn't mean it would be easy. Even if they were accepting, and I sure hoped they would be, it's a damn hard thing to do, and you can't understand it fully unless you're like me.

"It's not a cat video," I finally said.

"Ooh!" Mom nearly yelped. "I love me some good gossip. Please share, Nick. Your father is awfully boring."

Dad swatted Mom on her butt with the spatula. "Boring, my ass. Or your ass. No, your ass is anything but boring. Oh, shame on me. The kids are here. Hi, kids. Doesn't your mother have a nice ass?"

Jen spit the juice she was drinking right out of her mouth. I laughed, too.

"George! Shame on you is right!" Mom snapped.

"Oh, Laura. Don't be a prude!" He joked back and smacked her on the butt with his spatula again.

She laughed, almost crying. "Stop it, you buffoon! I want gossip from our son."

"Are you sure he's my son? You do seem awfully fond of the mailman."

"You're in a mood this morning! Oh, don't listen to your father, Nick. Here. Some bacon for some gossip. So, who is the lucky girl?"

Jen gave me that look, that *be honest, you promised* look. Sometimes I thought she was actually older than me and not my younger sister. I had been avoiding this moment my entire life. I hadn't planned it out, wasn't sure if I ever would find the right time and make the right plan, but then again, sometimes things need to be said in spontaneity. The happiness from last night entangled me in a web of euphoria. Maybe this was the moment.

After Mom put bacon on my plate, I said, "Can I tell you guys anything? I mean, tell you something and you promise not to be mad?"

That caught their attention.

"Oh no." Mom sat down. "Did something bad happen?"

"No, no, nothing like that. But I haven't been . . . uh, completely honest." I bit my lower lip and held my breath.

Dad sat down at the table next to Mom after that comment. Oh shit, I thought. What I am doing and how am I going to do it?

I tried to think of the right words to say. Then an image of Derek entered my mind. I was doing this not only for me but also so I could be with THE ONE. Yeah, I know I'm only sixteen, but right now he is THE ONE and the only one. There's no way I'd give up a relationship with him to be a coward or to keep a secret or to "fit in." Not now, not ever again. I thought of his strength. What would Derek say?

"I don't know if this is the best time to say this. For a long time though, I kept wondering when the best time to say this would be. And today seems like the best day of any. I'm really happy, Mom. Dad, I've never been happier. I've never felt . . . so alive. I want to tell you all about it. I want to . . ." I paused. My throat went dry in an instant, and I took a sip of the juice. "I want to be honest. It's been . . . hard for me. Hard to find the right words and the right time to say them."

Mom and Dad glanced at one another.

"The most important thing for me though," I continued, "is that you have to promise . . . promise to . . ." *Fuck*, I thought. My eyes started to hurt. Those damn tears, tears I didn't think I'd have after such an awesome night started knocking on the back of my eye lids. "Promise to love me no matter what. The thing I'm most terrified of is that . . . that you won't want me anymore."

My stomach felt sick. Literally sick, like I could throw up any second. I could feel the juice tumbling in my stomach like volcanic acid. I held back the tears, for now, but they were peeking out from the corner of my eyes.

"Nick, unless you're a serial killer, I can't think of anything you could say that would make us love you less," Dad said. "And if you are a mass murderer, then we'll hide you and protect you." He said this with the most serious of faces, as if I was about to tell him I had actually committed murder.

"I think I'm in love," I said. Both Mom and Dad's shoulders dropped a foot, completely relaxed. I don't think that's what they expected to hear.

"Why didn't you start with that?" Mom asked, holding her face in her hand, clearly relieved that I was not a murderer.

"There's more," I continued, and they straightened up once again. If you've never had to do this, it's hard to understand. I know. I don't want to be weak, but those tears has formed an army in the corners of my eyes and were ready to march to battle.

I looked at Jen. She moved closer to me and held my hand. I looked at her and the tears started falling down my cheeks. "I love you," I told my sister.

"I love you, too," she said and she started crying too. She hugged me then and cried on my shoulder.

"Oh, God, Nick, what is it? You're killing us right now," Mom stated, her face panicking.

"What is it, son? You can tell us anything," Dad added, obviously confused and worried as well.

"Mom," I choked out in between tears. I looked down, still trying to think of the right words. I had the phone on my lap still, and Derek texted right at that moment. In response to my text about singing, he wrote, *You sang on the way home? I sang in my sleep. Pretty sure I killed some angels. My singing voice is atrocious. But I've never woken up so happy.* I laughed out loud after seeing that text pop up on my phone.

"Oh, Nick, you're worrying us. What is it?" Mom asked again.

I never exhaled so hard, and then I sucked up the tears and silenced my laugh. I looked right at Mom and Dad, my eyes red and painful. "What I have to tell you . . . what is so important . . . is . . . that . . . I'm gay."

Silence can be more painful than words in such moments of vulnerability. My parents looked at me, then at each other. I looked over at Jen, who turned from me to our parents, waiting desperately on what they would say next.

Mom opened her mouth but Dad put his hand on hers and said to her, "Let me?" Mom smiled at him, and Dad said, "Nick. Oh, my son." He looked like he was now struggling for words, but instead of talking, he stood up and walked around the table. He pulled me up out of my chair and hugged me harder than he had hugged me ever before.

"I love you, Nick," Dad said. "I will love you who love. It's terrible we live in a world where you have to be scared to be who you are because there is absolutely nothing wrong with who you are."

Mom was crying now, but she stood up, walked around the table, and hugged me. "Oh, Nick. I'm not crying because you're gay. I'm crying because you are happy, and I am so happy for you."

They held me tightly. Jen was still by my side, and she joined also joined in. "I love you all," I said.

Dad pulled away and looked at me intensely in the eyes. "I can't imagine what worries and what pain you have felt. I am sorry for all of the idiots that have created a world where a child is worried about telling his parents what you told us. We will love and support you always."

"Thank you, Dad." I hugged him again.

"The same goes for me," Mom said. "The only pain I feel right now is from how long you've felt like you had to keep this a secret. I love you, baby."

"I love you, too, Mom."

"I love you, too!" Jen shouted.

"And of course, I love you." I hugged Jen back. I thought of all the stories I had heard about kids who weren't accepted by their families, and in this moment, I felt so lucky.

We hugged and held on to one another for several moments. Mom and I both wiped tears from our eyes, and we sat back down.

"So, you already had told Jen?" Mom asked.

I looked over at my sister, my best friend who I hoped would never grow up. "Somehow she knew. I don't know how she knew, but she did."

"He's my big brother. Sometimes I think I can feel what he feels. That's all," Jen said matter-of-factly.

"Son," Dad said. "There's a lot to talk about, and we want to know everything. But there are a couple of things I need to say now. First, we want you to be able to tell us everything. It's going to be a learning journey for all of us, but please never hold back again." He looked at Mom who nodded and then turned back to me. "That's not who we are. We may not always completely understand everything you feel, but we will never judge and we will always try to help when we can. Second, the world is getting better. I mean, more accepting, you know? But still, I see a lot of stupid people. Just the other day your mother and I were driving and noticed a couple not much different from us with a bumper sticker that read 'marriage = one man and one woman.' I told Mom then that I don't get that. Love is love, and why would anyone waste energy fighting something that doesn't affect them and doesn't hurt them and, contrary to whatever screwed up lessons they were taught, is completely natural. That's how I honestly feel. But there are mean people out there. Sometimes they hide it well. I just want you to be prepared for that and to know that we will be here for you then, too."

"I know, Dad. Thanks." I rubbed my eyes, finally now dry.

"You look so happy," Mom said. "I want to hear all about the boy."

"Can I ask something? Did you ever know or ever suspect that I was gay?"

Mom turned and smiled at Dad. "It's a conversation parents will have. Some will worry and say, 'Oh, Lord, what if our child was gay?' And then they'll try to pray the gay away if they suspect anything. We only prayed that you'd be happy and safe. I promise you that's all we ever prayed."

"So, you didn't know?" I asked.

"Well," Mom laughed. "There was a time when I thought the only girls you were ever going to like were either Gilmore or Golden."

"You like those shows, too!" I defended.

Mom laughed. "Yes, I do. We used to watch them together, and I'd think to myself that I wouldn't care who you ended up loving in life as long as I never lost those moments. The ones where we could watch anything, talk about anything, laugh about anything."

"We won't, I promise."

"You're damn right," Mom said. "I'd never let that happen."

There was silence at the table for a few minutes. I looked over at Jen who was beaming with pride. She smiled at me, and I could almost hear her thoughts. *See! I told you they'd be cool!* I smiled back at her, and Dad finally said, "Now, the worst thing that has happened today is letting all of this bacon go uneaten and this delicious food get cold. Let's eat. And then we want to hear all about this guy, Nick. If he's won your heart, he's already won ours."

I almost cried again. The most rewarding things we say or do will never be easy, I thought. Thank God for my family.

"I would love some bacon," I said. My parents and my sister smiled, and we ate like heroes that morning. They were heroes. I only told the truth. They were the ones who had to react to it. It takes more than action to be a hero; it takes the right reaction, too.

"I did it, Derek!" I called him after a nice, long breakfast and told him everything that had happened.

"Congrats! I'm so happy for you. You have a great family."

"Yeah, it's nice. It's so weird though, you know? I was worried and dreading that moment for like ever. Now it's over, and everything is actually okay."

"Yeah, it's a relief."

"It's all because of you," I told him.

"I didn't do anything."

"Yeah, you did. It's one thing to know who you are and a whole different thing to know what it's like to . . . to really feel alive." I stared up at the ceiling in my bedroom, just chilling on my bed.

"You're very sweet, Nick."

"It's just the truth. So, you never did tell me the story about you and your parents." I rolled on my side and pictured Derek chilling right next to me.

"It's kind of depressing," he said.

"If you want to tell me, I would still care to hear it."

"Well, okay, I guess." He paused and it took a few moments for him to speak again. I wondered if I should have asked or should have waited for him to tell me, but then he continued. "Um, like I said, I told them the summer before my sophomore year. Like we know, we've always known who we are. Straight people like to ask 'when did you know?' Don't you ever want to ask, 'when did you know you were straight?' You just know, you always know. It's not a damn decision or a choice. I mean, look at us. Who would choose to go through this?" He sighed and I nodded, even though he couldn't see me. "We have to go through this because it's who we are. But anyway in junior high, I had a crush on a boy. We used to wrestle, but I'd get . . . you know, excited." I giggled at that, and I swear I could feel Derek smile back, too. Then he continued. "He felt it once and got all weird and mad at me, and we never hung out again. He was a good friend, and I felt pretty bad. When we were freshmen, he told that story. 'Careful around Derek. He'll get a boner and rub it all over you if you let him.' Everyone in high school knew that damn story, and my freshman year was hell. I had no friends. Although I played basketball in junior high, I never played as a freshman. I didn't try out. I was too embarrassed. I let a douche bag's insults define who I was. When that terrible year was over, I made a decision to never let that happen again. People are of course always going to judge you and me, but I decided I was going to have control over what they knew by being completely honest. It was like a makeover that summer. I thought long and hard about who I wanted to become and how to get there."

He paused for a moment, and I didn't interrupt him. He was very serious in his tone, and I enjoyed listening to his story. I rolled over on my back and closed my eyes, to completely soak up and picture his story.

"I started with my parents. I thought all of June about what to say and how to say it. On the first of July, I sat them down and came out. Nothing fancy or poetic. Straight and to the point."

He sounded like he was taking a drink of water. "Then what happened?" I asked.

"Dad was the worst. He said, 'You think about other men like that? I'm disgusted. How can you feel that way? It's unnatural and sick.' He stormed off and Mom cried. She looked like she didn't know if she should comfort me or comfort my Dad."

Another pause. "Oh, Derek, I'm sorry. That's terrible." I opened my eyes. They felt wet again, and my head hurt.

"Thanks. Dad hasn't spoken to me since then. My Mom and he fought all of July. By August, he moved out. By the end of that year, they got a divorce."

"How's your mom now?"

"I worry she blames me for breaking up her marriage. Of course, she did the right thing. He's a complete bigot. The kind of guy who a hundred years ago would be wearing a white sheet over his head and burning crosses in people's yards, you know? What bothers me about my mother is that she's never really told me that she's sorry for what an asshole my dad is. I get the vibe that she expects *me* to apologize to *her* for Dad leaving, like this is all my fault."

"Jesus." I blinked hard and let a tear roll down my cheek.

"And I think sometimes that she'd go right back to him the moment I move out of the house."

"Really?"

"She's very lonely and very depressed. She went to therapy to get on meds because of me. How twisted is that? *She* needed therapy because of who *I* was."

"That's fucked up." I shook my head in bed. *What is wrong with people?* I started to feel bad about telling Derek my story. My parents were awesome, and his . . . hid dad leaving, parents divorcing, and his mom seeking therapy? Jesus, that's messed up.

"Anyway, that's most of the story I guess. I spent the rest of that summer and the rest of that school year working on my jump shot, lifting weights, working out. Like I told you before, if no one else was really going to stand up for me, then I was going to become as strong as I could. Physically and mentally. When sophomore year started and we did introductions in class, I told everyone I was gay. I didn't make a big deal of it. I said, "Hi, I'm Derek, I like basketball, blah blah blah, and I suppose one unique thing about me is that I'm gay. And while I'm not the only one of course, I'm the only one I know so far who is out and comfortable. It's just who I am and I'd appreciate it if people accepted that.' The strangest thing is that most of my classmates were more accepting then my parents. No one said anything when I tried out for basketball, but I think they were nervous in the locker room. Of course, I had gotten good, really good, maybe the best on the team. They wanted to win more than they wanted to hate me. And that's the *Cliff's Notes* version of my story. How's that for a Sunday afternoon?"

"That's a lot." I sat up in bed. I wished I was by his side so I could hug him.

"Yeah, I guess it is."

I had questions. I wanted to know more about his parents. I wanted to know about his teammates and more about school and basically everything. I didn't want to push too much today though. He had shared a lot.

I did have one question though I had to ask. It's a question I'll always have, I think. "What do you think happened to your dad? I mean, what made him that way?"

"I think about that all the time," he said and paused for a moment. "I had a pretty good childhood. He'd take me out and we'd watch movies and play games together. Politically, I always knew he was an asshole. He liked Ted Nugent and Sarah Palin way too much. But I really hoped those were only crazy interests. I'm his son. His family. He might have enjoyed a talk show or politician who was crazy because that was just entertainment, right?"

"Do you think those things shaped his views?"

"No, I don't think so. I think he liked those things because they validated views he already possessed."

"So how did he get those views?"

Derek paused. I pictured him thinking, but it seemed like he had thought about this before. "The more I think about him, the more I realize that the people he admired were the ones who loved to hate. They understood fear, not acceptance. They understood hate, not love. They understood sin, not forgiveness. He sees one path, one way of being that is right, and every other path is wrong."

"But that's wrong."

"He'd tell you he's right."

"So his stubborn, bigoted attitudes: that's more important than family?" I squeezed my hands into fists.

"When you walk a very narrow path, you focus only on yourself."

"That's really sad." I wiped away another tear, hopefully the last tear of the day.

"Yeah. Yeah, it sure is," Derek said.

Chapter Fifteen

"Listen up!" Asantà shouted. He had organized a team meeting after practice on my behalf. We had a plan, and I was on a roll with this honesty thing. It was time.

"Nick has something to tell you all. I've already talked to Nick about all of this, and we decided this was the best approach. I expect you all to listen and to be respectful. We are a team, and we always will be no matter what."

We were gathered in the school's gymnasium. I asked not to do this in the locker room.

Toby, Jared, and Zack sat up front and the rest of the team behind them. I hadn't told them yet either, but I wanted to get in all done in one shot. It's true that once you start being honest, it gets a little easier to say each time, but all the emotions get exhausting. I don't always want to think about how to say things, how to come out, or worry about how people will react. Sometimes I just want to play basketball.

"Hey, guys," I said and Asantà took a seat next to Toby on the floor. "Asantà and I agree that a team should be honest with one another. That's not the only reason I want to talk to you today, though. We're more than a team. We're friends. If we're going to be friends, there's something I want to tell you."

Asantà nodded with encouragement, and I continued. "If I don't tell you, you'll hear from someone else eventually. So I want to be the first to tell you. Guys, um, you should know I'm dating someone from Mayville."

They looked confused, and I smiled. I was trying to ease my way into this. "I should be more specific. I'm dating an athlete from Mayville. A basketball player. Their best player. Derek Burka. He's my boyfriend."

A few players in the back mumbled something. Asantà snapped, "Shut up and listen."

"Yeah." I shrugged. "I like guys. That's what I needed to tell you. You'll see Derek at our games, and I'll be cheering him on, when we don't play each other, that is. You're my friends, and I want to be able to bring him along when we go out and be real with ya. This is as real as I can get. I'm gay. Always have been. Not a choice. Just who I am. To be honest, I'm kinda tired of talking about it. I just want to do all the things I've always done, but I understand that for some, this can be a shock, a little weird. It shouldn't be, but it is. Questions?" I took a deep breath. Everyone looked at me in silence. Some fidgeted. I thought to myself that all of this shit has aged me like ten years in a week. Never thought I'd have to do all this just to be me.

"How can you, Nick?" Zack spoke up. "How can you date the enemy?" Then he stood up and laughed.

Toby added, "Yeah, man! How are you gonna play him if we rematch?"

"I'll wear extra tight shorts and distract him," I joked.

They laughed a little awkwardly, but it was cool.

"Careful," Jared said. "You might distract a few of us too." He smiled.

"Everyone okay?" Asantà asked. The team nodded. "Good, because this is okay. Nothing changes. Nick's got a boyfriend and a hell of an eye on the court. He's my best friend and always will be, and if I hear any homo jokes, you'll have to deal with me." The team nodded again. "All right, go home, we all got other shit to do."

Toby, Jared, and Zack hung around after the team left. "So," Zack asked, "is he better at giving head than Darcie?"

"Don't be a perv!" I laughed. "We haven't done that yet."

"How long have you been together?" Toby wondered.

"A week. But I've known him a lot longer than that. It's a long story. I'll tell you all about it, if you want, I promise. I just need to know you're on my side."

"Dude, it's cool. What do you think we are?" Jared said.

"If anyone hurts you, we'll hurt them. We're a team," Toby stated.

"That's right," Asantà agreed. "And best friends. One of our friends likes a bro then we like that bro, that's how it's done."

"For sure," Zack said. "So we hanging tonight? Call of Duty?"

I smiled and relaxed. I know not everyone can be so lucky to have the friends and the parents I do, and I can't help but feel absolutely wonderful. "Yeah, I'm game," I said. "Let's kill some ten year olds."

They laughed, and we left the gym together. Jared looked at me and grinned. "You're a son a bitch, you know that? You got the girl first and now you got the guy you want, and I can't even get a date. It's not fair."

"It'll happen, man."

"You think so?" he asked.

"I know so."

✳✳✳✳✳

It may appear awkward to anyone who wasn't us, but I had asked Darcie to go Christmas shopping with me to get Derek a gift.

"How are you guys doing?" she asked.

"Good," I replied. "Thanks for coming with me. I hope it's not weird."

"If we're going to be friends, going shopping for one another's significant others shouldn't be weird." Then she laughed. "But yeah, it's a little weird."

"Thank you for being a friend."

"Been watching *The Golden Girls*? Geez, you are gay," she joked.

"The guys would be terrible at this, you know. I need someone with taste." She smiled at the compliment, and we walked through the mall, looking for the perfect gift.

"So what are you looking for?"

"We've only been together a month now, so I guess nothing too crazy. Something fun."

"Just fun?"

"Well, something fun but if you look closely enough it will also say 'I love you.' Is that lame?" I asked.

"No, it's sweet." She sighed and I wondered if she was jealous. She had to be, even if just a little, right?

"Good. That's exactly what I want then." We browsed shop after shop, looking at T-shirts, random pop culture gifts, movies, books, and I couldn't make up my mind.

"Tell me your story again. The story of how you first met him," she said.

"Are you sure?" We had talked several times, and I had told her bits and pieces, but I was trying to be aware of how she might feel. I didn't want to say I fell in love with him while we were still together.

"I know it's weird, Nick, and I can't promise it doesn't upset me." She bit her lower lip. "But I also know that it's not something you could exactly, like, control. I'll get over it. If we're going to be friends, I want to know everything. Tell me."

I started with the bus ride, but I left me faking falling asleep to touch him. I talked about the roller coasters, the hot day, the lion he won me playing a basketball carnival game.

"All I can tell you," Darcie replied with a sigh, "is what I would love to receive if I were a part of that story."

I gave her a half-smile. I knew this wasn't exactly easy for her. "You're the best for this, you know?"

"I know. And you owe me. Just remember that. One day I may need you, okay?"

"Deal." As long as you don't ask me to go DOWN THERE ever again. I held back a smile at my own thought. "So what do you think?"

"You should get something that reminds you of that first day. A stuffed animal like he won you. A book about theme parks. Maybe even a toy basketball hoop. Something like that."

"Yes!" I thought for a moment. "Yeah, that gives me the perfect ideas. You're a genius," I cheered and hugged her.

"Yeah, yeah, you appreciate me now." She frowned.

I pulled away and paused. "Will you always make little jabs like that at me?"

This time she gave me a forced half-smile. "For now. Just deal. I still love you, though."

"Fair enough. Okay, help me look for a book."

We went to Barnes & Noble, and I went straight to the travel section to find what I was looking for: a great book that ranked the best roller coasters in the world with thrilling pictures and full descriptions. It was perfect.

We waited in line to be rung up. The store was crazy busy for Christmas, but finally a sweet-looking, older woman called "next."

"Hi," she greeted. "Is this for your girlfriend here?"

Darcie laughed. "I'm not his girlfriend."

"Aww, forgive an old lady. You two look so cute together. Sorry if I'm nosy. It keeps me entertained at work."

Darcie looked at me and I gave her a nod and a smile that said "say what you want." I really didn't care. I really didn't want to care.

"It's for his boyfriend, actually."

"Well isn't that something," the lady said. "My two sons always loved amusement parks. Never grew out of it."

"Do either of them have boyfriends?" I asked without thinking. The question flowed out of my mouth. I don't know why I asked.

"Oh heavens no. Thank God I didn't have to deal with that. That will be $28.50. Cash or charge?"

She didn't mean any harm. I knew that. But do you see how far we have to go? So many parents worry if their children may turn out gay, like it's a disease. They think "Thank God I didn't have to deal with that" when they meet someone who is gay, that they were "lucky" because they had straight kids who lived straight lives.

I bit my lip and it hurt, but not as much as her random comment hurt me. In that moment, it dawned on me why there are pride parades and other celebrations of gay culture. If we don't celebrate who we are, who will?

*****

I can't remember ever being more excited for Christmas. When you're a child, it's all about the gifts you'll receive. Over time, post-Santa Claus, it becomes kind of the same commercialized holiday over and over. I remembered being very proud the first time I saved up my allowance, money from my parents, to buy them a gift. They were essentially getting a gift with their own money. It was fun though, and I was always excited to see their reactions. After a few years, that kind of became routine, too. This year was the first time I was buying a Christmas present for someone I loved who wasn't an immediate family member. It was the most excited (and scared, if I'm being honest) I had ever been for Christmas.

"What do you and your mom do for Christmas?" I asked Derek on the phone that night before I went to bed.

"We usually go to my grandparents. Her parents. My dad goes to his parents' house. I don't get to have a relationship with them."

"That sucks."

"It does." I pictured him frowning.

"So when will you see your grandparents on your mom's side this Christmas?"

"I think we're leaving in the morning. A noon meal. Followed by hours of awkward conversation avoiding anything about my father or my sexuality. I wish you could come. If you were there, I'd have fun. What does your fam do?"

"We try to go to both grandparents' houses in one day. It's exhausting. Mom's parents in the morning. Then Dad's later that day. Do you guys do anything Christmas Eve?"

"Mom will probably drink herself into a coma and watch Christmas movies. So, no." He laughed.

"We always have done a small Christmas Eve dinner, just my parents, me, and my sister. It's my favorite actually. The main fam, you know? No travelling, no rushing. So . . . you're free Christmas Eve?"

"Unless mom lets me drink with her. And even if she did, I'd pass. Talk about depressing." I pictured him rolling his eyes and I smiled.

"Will you come over?" I asked.

"On Christmas Eve?"

"Yeah. You can have dinner with us. It's totally cool. And then after, you and I can just hang."

"Nick," he said, "you just made me excited for Christmas."

"So, that's a yes?"

"That's a hell yes!"

*****

You're probably wondering what all Derek and I had been doing since we started dating. It's cool. It's only natural to be curious since we're the hottest, sweetest couple in the world. We didn't get to see each other on school nights, but we texted all day long and talked every single night before bed. Sometimes for hours. We didn't even need things to talk about. Sometimes we'd just play music. He'd tell me of a favorite song, and I'd listen to it on my computer and keep him on the phone at the same time. Afterwards, I'd tell him what I thought of the song and give him something to listen to as well. Or we'd watch the same TV shows, but keep each other on the phone so we could laugh together or make random comments at each other. It was great.

We hung out in person every Friday and Saturday that we didn't have a game. Usually, it was one night or the other. We had games almost every weekend.

I can feel where your mind is going. You want to know the dark and dirty details. Sorry to disappoint you, but we hadn't done anything but kiss. We kissed a lot, let me tell you. But we were cautious, maybe even scared.

"Are you a virgin?" he asked one night on the phone.

"Are we doing the whole sexual history now?"

"I think it's good to know about one's past before going further, yeah, if that's cool."

"It's cool," I said. I wanted to do more with him. If this would help, then I was definitely game. "Well, I've kissed one other guy besides you. Mostly out of curiosity. But it was nothing like kissing you."

"What about the girls you were with?"

"There's only Darcie. We came close."

"How close?"

"You want every detail?"

"No. I don't think so, anyway." He laughed. "I'm just curious."

"She did some things to me. Hands and one time mouth."

"What did you do to her?" Was that curiosity? Or did I detect some jealousy in his voice?

"Mostly I sat scared out of my mind."

"Mostly?"

"One time she pushed me to return the favor. I started to do so, but I got sick. For real. I hope that's not weird to hear."

He paused for a moment. I held my breath while waiting for his reply. "No, I like knowing about you. Even if I'm jealous."

"Don't be jealous. I got through it . . ." Should I tell him this? It was the truth. "I got through it by picturing you."

"Seriously?"

"For real. And that was before I even really knew you."

"You're crazy."

"You make me crazy."

"I wouldn't be asking you these questions if you didn't make me crazy, too," he told me.

"So what about you? What are your experiences?"

"Nothing with a girl. Never had a girlfriend. When I came out, I dated one guy for a bit. He was a junior when I was a sophomore."

Now I felt jealous and sick. Maybe I didn't want to hear this. Maybe I had to. "What did you guys do?"

"We made out a few times. That's all."

I breathed a sigh of relief. "What happened to you two?"

"He was gay and I was gay, and that was the only reason we were together. He seriously asked one night at his house if I wanted to jerk off with him to porn. It was so direct, it was a turn-off. I told him I can jerk off to porn anytime I want. There just wasn't much to him except for a sex drive and too many pimples."

I laughed. "He sounds nasty."

"He was."

"I'm glad you told me. I had been thinking of asking if you wanted to watch some porn together," I joked. "Now I know I'd better be careful."

"I'd say yes if it was you asking."

"Yeah?" If you could only have seen my smile . . . Damn, this was one of the times I wish he lived closer.

"No doubt."

"Maybe we will someday." I swallowed hard.

"I hope we'll do lots of things someday."

I had been sitting in bed, and I looked down. I was as hard as a surfboard. I didn't tell him that or what I did after we hung up and said good night, but I'm not ashamed either.

*****

Christmas Eve came next, and I was thrilled to have Derek finally meet my parents and my sister. Perhaps thrilled wasn't the best word. I may have been excited, but I was also sick and nervous as hell.

He arrived right on time, as I had expected, and I answered the door and hugged him before he could get a word out. "I'm so happy you're here."

He smiled and kissed me.

"Oh, what is all that?" I asked at the presents he brought with him.

"It's not Christmas without gifts. I got something for everyone."

"You're fucking amazing. Come inside."

Mom and Dad and Jen were dancing with anticipation in the living room. I really thought their muscles were about to burst out of their skin.

"Hi," Derek greeted them, but before he could get another word, Jen ditched our parents and charged at him. She wrapped her arms around his waist and hugged him as hard as she had ever hugged me.

"My brother has never been this happy," she told him. "For that, I love you already. But if you ever make him sad, I will find at least a dozen ways to kill you. Did he tell you I'm smart? Because I am and I will find the best way to kill you."

Derek laughed and hugged her back. "I wish I had a sister like you." She smiled at him, satisfied with the compliment, and let Mom and Dad introduce themselves.

"I'm George," Dad said and reached out his hand. Derek shook it, and Dad continued, "You are more than welcome here. Any time. We are very pleased to meet you."

"Thank you, sir. It is a privilege to meet you." Dad nodded, and it was Mom's turn.

Like daughter like mother, she wasted no time with an introduction or handshake. She wrapped her arms around Derek and pulled him in tight. "You're gorgeous!" she said. "That'd be enough to win me over! But so polite and charming, too. Oh, Derek, so nice to have you here. Please, make yourself at home. Are you hungry?"

"Starving, ma'am, thank you."

"Ma'am? Am I an old lady? You call me Laura or you get out." She laughed.

"Yes, Laura, thank you."

I looked at my family and wondered if I was dreaming. Mom and Dad were smiling, not tolerating, not only accepting, but freakin' happy to have Derek here. *Happy*. Jen came back and grabbed Derek's hand.

"I want to show you my room!" she said. "And I'll tell you every secret about Nick there is!"

"That sounds like the best night ever," Derek said.

"Jen!" I called. "You be good."

"It's gonna be better than good!" She giggled and pulled Derek away.

The two of them were gone, and it was me and my parents left in the room. Mom came close and whispered, "Oh, honey, he really is gorgeous. And so sweet. Oh, I'm so happy for you!"

"Thanks, Mom."

Dad tried to joke too. "I know we've talked about this, Nick. You're born gay. It's not a choice. Are you sure? I'm having second thoughts on my life choices after meeting him."

"Dad, you're nuts."

"I'm just happy for you, kid." He laughed and rubbed my head. "And so happy you invited him over." Then he grabbed me tight around the shoulders and pulled me close and hugged me.

"We love you," Mom said and hugged me, too.

"You guys, thanks. But c'mon, now. Don't suffocate him or embarrass me."

"Me?" Mom cried. "Not me. Hey, Derek! Come back here! Want to see nude pictures of Nick when he was a kid? I have tons!"

*****

Minus the fact that Derek saw me naked before I wanted him to see me naked, even if they were only pictures of me as a young child playing in the bath, the night went incredibly well.

After a great dinner, he said, "I have something for you all. Is now a good time?"

"It's always a good time for presents!" Jen cheered.

"Okay, give me a minute, please." Derek went and got the gifts he had brought with him. "I'm taking a wood shop class at school. It's nothing fancy, but I wanted to bring something for all of you. This is for you both," he said to my parents and gave them a long, rectangular gift wrapped in a blue, red, and white snowman theme.

"Oh, Derek, you're something else," Mom said, taking the gift. My parents unwrapped it together. "Oh, it's beautiful. I don't know what to say. It's absolutely beautiful."

It was a wooden, rectangular art piece with an engraving. Dad read it aloud. "It says, 'Family: those who accept and love unconditionally.' Derek," Dad paused, and I thought I saw him choke up. "Derek, thank you. It's perfect and very well made. You should be proud."

"You should be proud, sir," he said. "You have a wonderful son and daughter." He turned to Jen and handed her a gift, too. "I hope you like it," he said.

She unwrapped it ferociously. It was similar to our parents' gift, but more of a square then a rectangle. He had engraved a female superhero in the center and all around it, he had written: "Sisters are the real superheroes."

Jen hugged Derek again. "I love it! How did you know?" She laughed.

"Your brother has told me a lot about you, and from what I know, you are a real superhero."

She kissed him then, on the cheek, and looked at me. "I take back what I said earlier. If you ever make him sad, Nick, I will find a hundred ways to hurt *you*!" She took her gift and held it tight against her chest. "This is going up right above my bed. Dad, will you help me hang it?"

"Of course, sweetie," he said.

"I'm glad you like it. I have one more gift. For Nick." He paused then and looked at me as if trying to send me a thought telepathically. I think I understood.

"Guys, do you mind if we excuse ourselves?" I asked.

Mom looked at Dad, who nodded, then back at me. "We need to clear the table and clean up anyway. Yes, of course. Thank you for your sweet gifts, Derek. We'll give you two time to yourselves now, okay?" Mom said.

"Thanks, Mom," I said. "We'll go upstairs."

We went up to my room. "I don't know what potion you drank tonight," I told Derek, "but you are magical. You won over my entire family."

"I'll do whatever it takes to get you alone." He grabbed me and kissed me hard, pulling me in as closely as possible. I tried to sink into him even deeper, kissing him with every ounce of spirit I had. I pushed him into my bedroom wall, making enough noise to worry me for a brief moment, but I kept on kissing him harder and harder.

He pulled away. "I need to breathe, sorry." He laughed. "And I have a gift for you, too, of course." He handed me the last of the presents he had brought with him.

I tore the gift open with the same enthusiasm as my sister. "Oh my God. How did you get this?"

"I made the frame myself," he said quietly.

I stared at his gift in total awe. It was a picture of us on a roller coaster from last summer, both of our hands up, our mouths screaming in pure excitement and happiness.

"You went to the bathroom after one of the rides that day we met. When you left, I secretly bought one of the pictures they took of us."

"It's amazing," I said. "Wow. This is the first day we met. I don't think I've been that happy. Until today."

"You like it?"

"I love it. Thank you." I kissed him again. I wanted to say 'I love you' but I hoped my gift would do that for me. I pulled away and handed him my present.

"I got something for you, too."

His gorgeous smile made me feel like the only person in the world. With great energy, he ripped apart the wrapping paper.

It was the book on roller coasters. "Oh, how cool!"

"Read the inscription," I said.

He opened the book to the first page where I had written a personal message. He read it aloud. "You are my roller coaster, and I hope the ride never ends. I love you—Nick."

He kissed me then and told me, "I love you, too."

"Not as much as I love you."

"That's one fight I'll have with you. I love you more."

We kissed and he pushed me against the wall this time. Each kiss was better than the last, and each "I love you" was spoken more passionately than the previous one.

I hoped it would always feel this way.

Chapter Sixteen

Asantà's parents, trusting him too much, were going out of town for a New Year's Eve party, and when he heard that great news, he texted all of us: *NYE party at my crib!*

We hadn't drank in the longest time, not since Halloween, and we asked Jared if he could score some liquor again from his older brother.

"Shouldn't be a prob. Especially since it's New Year's. What should we get?"

"No Jack!" I grunted. "Something sweeter, please."

"Ha, I'll see what I can do."

"Can I invite Derek?" I asked Asantà.

"Course." He paused for a moment. "You cool if I, uh, invite Darcie?"

What could possibly go wrong with having my ex-girlfriend and my boyfriend in the same room, especially if there was a lot of alcohol to go around? "Yeah, of course. The more, the better, right?"

"Hell yeah. We need to get a few more girls here for the guys."

"What's with you and Darcie?" I asked.

"She's hot, man. You know that. Is it weird for you if I like her?"

I shrugged. "It shouldn't be. But yeah, a little."

"I was thinking of asking her out."

I saw this coming on some level, but I had also been pretty distracted recently. Darcie had become a great friend, and Asantà was my best friend. It was weird for a couple reasons, but I wasn't going to let Asantà down. "You only live once. Go for it."

"Thanks, man." He held up his fist, and I bumped it. "Okay, help me think of some girls to invite for the other guys!"

The more I thought about New Year's, the more excited I got. We had a house to ourselves, we'd have beer and liquor for everyone, it wouldn't matter how loud our music was, and I'd have someone to kiss at midnight. And I could do all of this in front of my best friends and even my ex. Okay, it was a little strange, but whatever.

Derek picked me up, but of course my parents and Jen wanted to see him before we left.

"Look where we put your gift," Mom said and pointed to the wall in the living room that also held some family portraits. "It goes perfectly there."

"I'm glad you like it, ma'am. I mean, Laura." She smiled and hugged him.

"Mine is in my bedroom!" Jen said. "Wanna see?"

"Of course." She took his hand and dragged him to her room, where Dad had helped hang her gift above her bed.

"Nick, so, is there going to be booze at this party?" Dad asked.

"That goes without saying, I think, George," but Mom gave me a wondering look, too.

"I'll be careful, I promise."

"That doesn't answer my question," Dad said. "Will there be booze?"

"Yeah, probably."

"You know that makes us uncomfortable," Mom said. "And his parents are gone? Nick, you're only sixteen."

"It's just a few of us. Didn't you party at all when you were young?"

They looked at one another and shared an awkward chuckle that hinted at dozens of great stories. "I want you to check in twice." I started to speak up but Mom snapped at me, "TWICE. Once before midnight and once after midnight. Call, don't text. I want to hear your voice and know you are okay."

"Okay. Thank you for letting me go."

"We know it's important for you to have good times with your friends. Just be safe." Dad paused a moment here and then added, "And that also goes for Derek. You know we like him. Be safe. Make good choices."

"I will. Of course." My cheeks reddened as I wished for Derek to come back before they said anything else.

Footsteps and laughter echoed from the hall, and Jen appeared, still holding Derek's hand. "Derek," Dad said, "you keep my son in line tonight okay? We trust you."

"Gee, thanks, Dad." I rolled my eyes but smiled.

"No problem, sir. I'll make sure I hold him when he does keg stands."

"Derek!" I nearly chirped, surprised.

He held his hands up. "Kidding! Just kidding! We will be safe, I promise."

"Okay. Have fun tonight," Dad said. "Not too much fun. And call. At least twice."

"Thanks, Dad. Bye, Mom. Bye, Jen. Happy New Year!"

*****

We arrived at Asantà's around eight that evening. The music was already pumping throughout the house. We headed to the basement. "Let's keep things down here. Less to worry about when my parents get back tomorrow night," he said.

"Shots, shots, shots!" echoed through the speakers. The guys were all there: Jared, Toby, and Zack. We had two cases of beer, and a couple of bottles of some liquor called Rumchata. "My brother says it won't kill us like Jack." He laughed. "And that it actually tastes good."

"What are we waiting for?" Toby asked. "Pour some shots!"

"Hey, Derek," Zack greeted. "Glad you made it, man. Welcome!"

"Thanks. Me, too."

Asantà added, "Yeah, welcome. Do a shot with us?"

"Sure." Derek smiled. I didn't know if Derek had ever drank before, not that I had a lot of experience.

We poured six shot glasses of the Rumchata. "To the New Year!" Jared toasted. We clinked our shots and tossed them back.

"Wow," Toby yelled. "It's like the milk after Cinnamon Toast Crunch. That's amazing."

"This could be dangerous," Zack said. "Liquor that tastes that good. Very dangerous."

"Yeah, let's not get sick like the last time," I suggested.

"Hey, I think that must be the girls!" Asantà said after hearing the doorbell.

"Girls? As in plural?" Jared asked, confused.

"You wait and see!" Asantà told him.

He ran upstairs, and it was Darcie who, with Asantà's help, had recruited three female friends to join us for the night. Asantà led them all down to the basement.

"Gentleman," he announced. "Let me introduce our other guests. You all know Darcie. These are some other of her friends. Amanda, Gabby, and Patrice. Ladies, these are my best friends. Toby, Zack, Jared, and Nick. And that's Nick's boyfriend, Derek."

The girls smiled and waved, and the three single guys wasted no time making new friends. Jared was the first and introduced himself again to Amanda. "Can I get you a beer?"

"Yes, thanks," Amanda said.

Toby introduced himself to Gabby. "You're in my history class, right?"

"Yeah. I sit by the windows, on the other side from you."

"Cool. Glad you could make it." Toby turned to Asantà and silently mouthed, "HOT" followed by "THANKS." Asantà grinned and nodded.

Zack then introduced himself to Patrice. "I've seen some of your games," she said to him. "You're very good."

"Thank you," and he took her to get a drink.

"Okay, guys, now that everyone knows everyone, let's get this party started! I've got a deck of cards and a list of drinking games. Get your drinks. Let's get crazy!" Asantà shouted. He turned up the music, everyone grabbed a beer, and we gathered in a circle on the floor. Then we drank and drank a lot.

*****

It didn't take long for the giggles and the dancing to kick in. Everyone was laughing at nothing, and then everyone was laughing at Jared attempting to do the robot dance. "No man, it's like this," Zack said and jumped up.

"Watch me whip!" Toby yelled. I don't know what he was doing or if it any way resembled the song he was attempting to emulate, but it was pretty hilarious.

It was about an hour until midnight, and Asantà and Darcie were talking privately in the corner after several drinking games. The other guys were trying to impress the girls by making fools out of themselves. I turned to Derek, who was still sitting on the floor next to me.

"Are you having fun?"

"Yeah. Your friends are crazy. It's entertaining."

"You feeling okay?"

"Yeah, it's cool." He belched a little and then giggled. "Sorry. I've never been drunk. The shots from the drinking game are messing with my head." He laughed.

I looked up and saw Asantà and Darcie kiss. Derek noticed and asked, "Is that weird for you?"

"No. I mean, a little. I don't know why it should be. It's just strange. My best friend and my ex-girlfriend. Is that weird for you?"

"Yes." He laughed. "But only because I'm jealous she knew you first." I kissed him then but pulled away a little too quickly. I looked around the room. This was the first time I had kissed Derek in front of any of the guys. I wondered if it would be weird for them.

"You worried what they'll think?" he asked.

"No. I mean, a little." I sighed. *Damn, I'm repeating myself.* "It's just a first. That's all."

"Then give them a first worth remembering," he said, grabbing me and pulling me close. He kissed me with the same passion from Christmas Eve, and I didn't let go this time. We must have been like that for minutes.

Finally, Jared said, "You guys! Thirty minutes till midnight. Time for more shots!" He poured several shot glasses full of Rumchata, and I looked around, curious for any reactions. Darcie smiled at me, and the other guys were too obsessed with the girls. No one noticed or no one cared.

I stood up and had to put my hand on the wall. "Wow, I guess I've been sitting a while. I didn't realize I was this dizzy." I laughed. Derek stood up a little shaky, too. He stumbled as we walked over to the table of shots, and he looked even cuter, if possible, with a new lack of coordination. I put my arm around his shoulder to help, leaned in, kissed him, and said, "I love you." I didn't care who would hear.

Zack and Toby saw and smiled. They looked like they wanted to crack a joke, or perhaps that was only my perception, but they held it in.

"Everyone got a shot?" Jared asked, looking around and double checking. "Okay, what should we cheer to?"

"To friends," Asantà said.

"To the best friends," I added.

"Yes, to best friends. Cheers!" Zack shouted. We tried to clink glasses, but lots of Rumchatta was getting spilled.

"Just drink," Jared said. "Alcohol abuse!"

We all grabbed another beer. "Have one ready for midnight!" Asantà told us. We all stood up, the music playing loudly, the girls starting to dance.

"I'm a terrible dancer," I told Derek. "But this is nice."

"Let me show you some moves." He grabbed my hands and spun me in circles.

"What do you call that?" I asked. "The make-Nick-throw-up dance?"

"Ha! I've got more!" He smiled wide, those shiny white teeth nearly glowing in the darkened room. "How about this?" He brushed his shoulders in a sweeping motion, lowering his body to the floor like he was doing the limbo at the same time.

"What do you call that?"

"Um . . . " Derek had to think about it. "The walrus!"

"Nice. I like that one." He grabbed me then, partly for balance, partly to hold me, I think. He got even closer and whispered something in my ear that I couldn't really hear because of the music. "What was that?" I asked. He whispered again. My eyes doubled in size. "Let's wait till after midnight, and then maybe we can sneak upstairs." His smile stretched from ear to ear, and he put his head against mine, holding me like we were slow dancing.

"You're perfect," he said.

"No. But you make me want to be."

*****

The countdown began, and we turned on the TV to watch the ball drop on Time's Square. Asantà held his phone in his hand as he counted down. "I've got the perfect song for midnight." He laughed. "I expect you all to get crazy!"

We yelled with the timer on TV. "Ten, nine, eight, seven, six, five, four, three, two, one! Happy New Year!"

I grabbed Derek and kissed him, and he returned my passion. It was deep and wet and full of love. We turned around and everyone was cheering, drinking, and making out. Asantà pulled away from a kiss with Darcie and smiled at me. "To us, Nick!" Some beer spilled as we tapped our cans together and took a sip. Asantà bro-hugged me, and then he turned to Derek. He bro-hugged him, giving him the one arm pat on the back. "Happy New Year, bro."

"Happy New Year." Derek returned the slightly awkward bro-hug.

The other guys were getting lucky, too. Everyone had someone to kiss at New Year's. Asantà hit play on the song he selected, and even if it was old and over-played, we screamed and shouted, "Turn down for what!"

The basement thumped with the bass of the music, and every couple was either dancing or kissing. Derek looked at me. "Now?"

"Now." We took this time to sneak upstairs. It felt inappropriate and gross to go into Asantà's parents' room, so we made our way to the living room. We stood in front of the couch, and he pulled up my shirt with the ferociousness of drunken love and kissed my chest. I arched my back, moaned, and felt instantly aroused. I didn't have to look down to know it was more than a feeling. I pulled him close and took off his shirt, and we kissed bare chest to bare chest, rubbing each other's backs, feeling the hardness of our pecs and the smoothness of our stomachs.

He moved back from me for a moment. His perfect smile complimented his excited eyes, and looking at him and feeling him made my heart beat harder than any moment before.

"Asantà wouldn't be mad if he saw us, would he?"

"No, I think he'd be proud." I grinned.

What he did next I had been dreaming of forever. He unbuttoned by jeans, pulled them down past my knees, and lifted one foot at a time to take them all the way off. I froze there in tight boxers with a throbbing erection. If he touched it, I may have exploded right there. But first, I needed to see him. Up until this moment, I had only imagined what was in his pants. I needed to see it. Needed to feel it.

I reached out and slipped him out of his jeans. He had on red boxer briefs, and I don't think I'll ever get that image out of my mind, and I wouldn't want to. He had a thick erection, reaching up toward his belly button, threatening to shred apart the threads that held his boxers together.

He grabbed me and we kissed again, feeling the literal force of our excitement against one another. It was one of the most exhilarating feelings, a hard proof symbol, pun intended, of our excitement.

He touched me then, over my boxers, and pulled ever so gently. I exhaled deeply and melted into his arms at the one touch. I had to feel him, too. Grabbing him over his boxers, I rubbed his penis, wanting nothing more now than to take off his underwear and put him in my mouth.

But the mutual touch was incredible, and when he kissed my neck, I understood what it meant to feel weak in the knees. I almost collapsed, but he held me up. When he took off my underwear, I couldn't physically stand any longer. I fell to the floor and took him with me, ravenously reaching for him and pulling off his boxers.

He followed me down, naked body against naked body, my back to the floor. He had one hand on my chest and one on my penis. One of my hands had found his dick, too, and it was hot and hard. My other pulled on the back of his neck to bring him closer.

I was going to explode. I couldn't hold it in, so I did the only thing I could think of to stop it for a moment. I pushed him over on his side and bent down and completely engulfed his dick in my mouth. He moaned and reached out again for mine. He grabbed on to it and pulled, and I sucked on him with as much passion as I possessed. "Nick," he said just as he grabbed my penis and I had really started going down on him, "I'm gonna cum." I took it all in my mouth and in that instant, he screamed and pulled on me harder. I tried to warn him, but my mouth was quite full. I came on his arm, his stomach, his chest. It shot everywhere.

I laid back down by his side. Our hearts were beating as hard as the music was thumping below.

I put an arm around him. "I love you."

"I love you, too," he said and smiled.

We laid there completely naked on Asantà's living room floor. I should get him a towel, I thought, but I didn't want to move. I didn't want to let go.

And sometime during that sweet—and somewhat sticky—embrace, we both fell asleep.

Chapter Seventeen

The next weekend Worthless High played the Burlington Bears. I didn't know much about Burlington, but I remembered them from my first date night with Derek. The guys who mocked us were starters on the Burlington varsity basketball team. I looked forward to getting some sweet revenge on the basketball court by kicking their asses.

Derek didn't have a game that night, so he was in the stands cheering me on. He was there with his best friend, a girl named Eliana who he had been friends with since grade school. He told me about her on our first date, but I still hadn't met her. Tonight was the night I'd meet his oldest friend, and from what he had told me about her, I was looking forward to it.

Back on the court, Jared faced Burlington's center for the tip off. The referee blew his whistle, tossed the ball straight up, and Jared tipped it over to me for possession.

I called out a play and dribbled down the court. Zack and Asantà switched positions and Toby cut across the midsection. I passed to Toby, who tossed to Asantà, who scored a beautiful jump shot. The first points of the game were ours, and I smiled as the Burlington players frowned.

One of the guys who mocked us that night I learned was named Jason, a forward for the Bears. The other was Michael, and he was their center. I wished I could have guarded one of them, but they were much taller than me. It turned out I wouldn't need them to taunt me that night. Ignorance must have spread throughout the whole team. The guy I was guarding, a junior named Frederick, wasn't any nicer than the teammates I had met on my first date with Derek.

"Stop staring at my balls, fag," he greeted me with his first possession down the court. I bit my lip. *Keep your head in the game. Beat him on the scoreboard, that's all that matters for today.*

He passed to Michael, who tossed it back out to Jason, who shot a perfect three. Damn.

Asantà took it out of bounds and passed to Zack this time. I ran down the court, Zack passed to me, Jared swung outside, and I faked to him and then threw it across to Toby near the baseline. He dribbled under the basket and hooked a layup.

Frederick took the ball back down the court. "You handle the ball well," he said to me. "But you've had a lot of practice handling balls, huh?"

Ignore, ignore, ignore, I repeated in my head. He smirked and then cut sharp to the left. I followed him hard and fast and ran smack into Jason who had set up a pick. He was a brick wall, and I fell. Frederick nailed a three, and Jason repeated his classy gesture from the night in the restaurant of pretending to suck on a penis.

"What's happening?" Asantà asked and helped me up.

"They're homophobic assholes. Derek and I ran into them a while back."

The game was neck and neck, and none of their players wasted an opportunity to insult me or try to make me fall, but I got up every time and kept my mouth shut. Asantà called a timeout near the end of the first quarter. Burlington had a six point lead, and Frederick had fouled me hard.

"You okay?" Asantà asked.

"Yeah."

"What's happening out there?" Coach asked.

"Coach, they're haters. They're insulting Nick every chance they have," Asantà said.

Coach frowned. He knew of course about me, but never made an issue about it. He focused only on basketball. But then he said, "Well, you're not gonna take it, you hear me? If they're gonna pick and foul you hard, you give back tenfold what they're giving to you. You're a team. Protect each other on that court, you all understand?" We nodded, and I felt like Rocky getting ready for a fight. This was no normal game. "Wasps on three," he said. "Now get them!"

I passed it to Asantà who drove hard right into Michael's face, scoring a layup and getting a foul shot on top of it. He made his free throw, and we cut their lead down to three.

"Nice!" I high-fived Asantà.

"That was for you."

"Give me the next one, guys," Jared said, his eyes glaring at the other team.

"You got it."

Frederick took the ball back down. "Feeling like a man? That must be a first." As he neared the three point line, he faked a pass and went for a shot. He shouldn't have said that. I was no longer in the mood to play nice. He went up for his shot, and I went to block hard. I slammed the ball out of his hands and right on his face. He went down.

The ref called a foul on me, and their team ran up. Jason pushed me from behind. "What are you doing, fag?" he yelled loud enough for everyone on the court to hear. I looked up at the stands, and Derek stood up with a concern written from head to toe.

The ref called a technical foul on him. "Watch your mouth and play the game. All of you," he warned us.

When the second quarter began, Zack passed the ball in to me, and I threw it hard down the court to Jared. Jared turned on Michael and dunked the ball in his face. Our cheering section roared. Their homophobia sharpened our skills, and by half-time, we were up by ten. Coach was proud, almost too proud, and told us to keep it up during the second half.

The third quarter went pretty smoothly. Their coach must have lectured them in the locker room and told them to keep their focus on the game and "not some fag," I imagined.

In the last few minutes of the game, they caught up, and we were tied, sixty-four points each. I had possession and called out a play. I tossed it to Asantà on the left, Zack set up a pick on my right, and I swung outside and cut down the middle. Asantà passed it to me, Jared picked Michael, and I went up for a layup. Out of nowhere, it felt, Jason came charging, jumped, blocked my shot, and hit me hard. His elbow jabbed my face, and I fell hard on the floor.

"Mother fucker," I heard, but it was Asantà cussing and he shoved Jason hard. He flew out of bounds, and Michael punched Asantà from behind in the back of the head. Jared grabbed Michael with all the strength of a giant, and I swear it was like a WWE move. Jared picked him up and body slammed him. I burst into laughter on the floor, even though my face hurt like hell.

Whistles blew. "Enough!" The refs had gathered around the fighting players, and forced the benched players from both teams, who had charged the court, to stay back.

They grabbed Asantà, Jared, Michael, Jason, and me. "You're all out of here! To your locker rooms until the game is over." I wanted to ask why I was included. *Did you not see me nearly knocked out on the floor?* But whatever.

The coaches replaced us, and Asantà, Jared, and I headed to our locker room. Coach actually smiled as we walked off, and I looked up at Derek, who was doing anything but enjoying the festivities. His eyes were wide with worry and he mouthed, "Are you okay?" I nodded and ran off the court.

"Those fuckers!" Asantà yelled and kicked at a locker.

"I can't believe that douche hit you from behind. Fucking coward. You okay?"

"Yeah, I'm fine."

"You should have seen the body slam Jared did on their center! I won't be surprised if you get recruited by the UFC after tonight!" We laughed and waited for the game to end. There were only a few minutes left, and when the team came in, they roared, and we knew they had won.

"Beat them by three in the end," Coach told us. "Nice work, team!"

The players gathered around the three of us who had been kicked out. "You guys okay?" Zack asked.

"Yeah," Asantà answered for us. "Even better that we won."

"I can't believe what dicks they are," Toby said.

"Me neither," I said. I sure wish I understood why, but I didn't. "Thanks guys for sticking up for me."

"We're a team, always. Plus, you know, it's the fucking right thing to do," Asantà said.

*****

Derek and his best friend Eliana were waiting for me after the game. When I came out of the locker room, he rushed up to me. "Jesus, are you okay?"

"I'm fine, I promise. A bruised face, maybe, but nothing else."

"Thank God," he said and hugged me. "I started to run down. I wasn't going to let them hurt you."

"He did," Eliana confirmed. "I had to grab him back. The refs broke it up pretty quickly."

"Thanks." I smiled.

"Hey, let me introduce you. Nick, this is my best friend Eliana. Eliana, well, this is Nick, obviously."

I reached out my hand and she said, "Turn around."

"What?"

"Just turn around."

I hesitated but obliged and did a full, slow spin for her.

"I had to double check that ass was real. It looked good in that uniform, but I had to be sure. Okay, I approve. He's got a great ass," she said to Derek.

"I agree," He laughed.

"So where should we go?" I asked.

"Steak 'n Shake?" he suggested.

"Fine by me," Eliana said. "Try not to start any fights in the restaurant, okay?"

*****

We drove to the closest Steak 'n Shake and got a table. Eliana was pretty. She was a little heavy, but not fat. She had long dark hair that covered her ears, a round face, and a bitchy smile. I liked her already.

"So, Derek tells me he's in love," she said after we ordered. I was surprised by how direct she was, but Derek seemed totally normal. He must be used to her.

"That's good," I said. "I feel the same."

"How many guys have you been with?" she asked.

"He's my first boyfriend."

"How many have you *been* with?"

"None, easy!" I put my hands up. "I kissed one boy before. That's it."

"He tells me you had a girlfriend," she stated. It wasn't a question so I wasn't sure what to say. "Hmmm." She just stared at me.

"Um, yeah. One girlfriend. Before I came out."

"You're only a junior. What are your plans next year?"

"I don't know."

"Hmmm. What about after high school? You thought of college?" Her eyes were narrow, and I felt like I was being interviewed by the Secret Service or something.

"I'm sure I'll go but I don't know where."

"And what if one of you goes far away to a different college? What then?"

"I don't know," I said. Damn, this was a little brutal. "We'll figure it out as we go. Listen, I love Derek, and it's a day at a time here, okay?"

She studied me, and I was beginning to feel uncomfortable. "Okay." Finally, she smiled. "Good enough for now. I'm just makin' sure you're not a player. Or just a perv." Her smile widened, and I relaxed.

"I'm pretty perverted, but I'm not a player," I told her. She laughed and nodded at Derek. I took that as a sign of approval.

And just as I was really beginning to relax, I said, "Fuck. Oh, fuck."

"What?" she asked.

"Is this the only damn place in town? Look who just pulled up." It was the Burlington High bus with the entire basketball team stopping for a team meal evidently before heading home.

"Do you want to leave?" Derek asked.

"We already ordered." I sighed and cracked my knuckles. "Let's just eat quick and go."

"Okay," he said. "Don't even look at them."

It's a lot easier said than done. They gathered in the back, and we tried our best to turn away from them in hope of not getting spotted.

"Thank God we don't go to that school at least," I told Derek.

Derek frowned. "I wish one of us did."

"What? Why?"

"You think we just got lucky with mostly tolerant schools and teams?" He looked at me, and if his voice didn't say it enough, his eyes sure were fired up. "The people at our schools and teams got better because of us. We're their friends. They saw what it really means to be someone like you and me." He looked over at the boys from Burlington. "That school—I bet no one is out. And no one will come out with assholes like them. The people who are most ignorant either never had a chance to really know someone different or intentionally chose not to get to know such a person. That's what makes people stupid."

I nodded. "Well, I'll just go over and ask if we can start over and be friends."

Eliana laughed. "I wouldn't do that yet."

"I was kidding."

"I know," she said. "Jesus, look at them. They even look dumb. *Hey, uh, why do they call it a steakburger? And why is it steak and shake? Do they shake the steaks? Why would they do that?* I can hear their intelligent conversations already."

We laughed and she added, "Well don't look now. They've spotted us."

"Shit," I said.

"They wouldn't do anything with their coach here, right?" Eliana asked.

"I don't know," Derek said. "He was pretty pissed they lost. He stormed into the locker room and cussed out the refs after the game."

"He probably thinks it's my fault his players got kicked out." I started to fidget with the silverware on the table.

"He's right," Eliana said, but she rolled her eyes. "I mean, you chose to be gay. His players certainly don't have any choice when it comes to hating you."

"It's a fucked up world, and I wouldn't be surprised if that's exactly what they thought," I said.

The server brought our food, but it sucked because we were eating so quickly and it was hard to enjoy the night out. "Fuck them," I said. "Slow down. Why should they get to ruin our meal?"

"You know what?" Elaina said. "I think I'm going to try every shake on the menu. We'll stay all night if we feel like it."

Right after she said that, Michael and Frederick got up and walked towards the bathroom, which of course had to be right by us.

"I guess girls always do go to the bathroom together," Eliana said loudly so they could hear.

Michael gave us the finger, and when they got closer, Frederick said, "We don't need to use the bathroom, fags. We just wanted to tell you to watch your backs." He grinned and I wanted to puke. "We'll give you what you like."

"Fuck off, losers. The short bus is calling," Eliana said.

"Bitches will get some too," Michael told her.

"Then I look forward to seeing what you get," Derek jumped in.

"Oopsy." Eliana picked up her shake and tossed its contents right at Michael's crotch. "Oh, I see you actually get excited seeing a couple of guys together. Look at the mess you made!" She laughed.

"Bitch!" Michael jumped back.

"C'mon," Frederick said. "They'll get theirs. Later. When the moment is right." Then they walked back to their table.

"I feel sick," I said.

"Yeah. They make me sick," Eliana added.

"I really hate them."

Eliana nodded.

"Can we just get out of here?" I asked.

"Yeah, let's go somewhere else," Derek said. We paid for our food, and as we left the restaurant, I looked over my shoulder. Frederick was waving at me with a mockingly limp hand, and the others laughed.

It was one of those moments where I simply wanted to go back in time and fit in and not be the guy who stands out and gets ridiculed. Derek reached out to hold my hand, and I hated myself even more: I pretended not to see it, stuck my hand in my pocket, and marched out quickly to get in the car.

Chapter Eighteen

It was one of those horribly boring weeknights. School had been slow, and practice had been hard. We were nearing the end of the season, and we only had one loss, the loss against Derek's Tornados. There would be another game against them soon, and although no one directly said anything, I could tell coach and the team were wondering if I should even play. Boyfriend against boyfriend in a game to see who'd take first place in our region.

I wasn't really thinking about that, though. I was home, staring at my computer, ignoring homework, and listening to random music. Derek texted a couple of hours ago, and I still hadn't replied to him.

It had been like this for a couple of weeks. I didn't know what I was feeling anymore. I loved him, don't get me wrong. But maybe it's hard to be sixteen and in love, with school and practices and parents and stupid people in the world who judge you. I wanted him. I dreamed of him and his body at night, but we hadn't been intimate since New Year's.

Mom knocked on my door. "Can I come in?"

"Yeah."

"How's the homework coming?"

"It's not."

"I see," she said looking at a pile of unopened books on my desk. "You doing okay?"

"Yeah."

"You don't sound very convincing."

"I don't know, mom." I opened a book and flipped through some pages without looking at them. "It's hard."

"What's hard?" She took a seat at the edge of my bed.

"Everything."

"It's hard being a parent, too, you know." She smiled gently. "We're happy when you're happy and we're sad when you're sad."

"I know."

"He's your first love. Statistically, you'll have lots of love in life. You're very young."

I closed the textbook. "It's not that, mom. I do love him. I know what people say about someone my age, but I don't care. It feels like he is the forever one." I looked her hard in the eyes. Sometimes I didn't understand the words coming out of my mouth. Fifteen-year-old Nick certainly didn't talk this way. Hell, I don't think I talked this way a few months ago, but Derek . . . well, he changed everything about me. Was that what was scaring me?

"So how do you feel right now?" Mom stood up and put a hand on my shoulder. "Do you not feel like that anymore?"

"No not at all. It's . . . hard to explain."

"I know, honey, but you can talk to me or Dad about anything."

I stared at the floor and mumbled, "If I love him, why do I feel so weird about everything now?"

She thought for a moment and scratched my back gently for a minute. "Sometimes we get what we want and then we start to doubt ourselves. Was this really what I wanted? Maybe we wonder if we deserve it. Or we see how it's changed us and we wonder if life wasn't simpler before. Do you ever think like that?"

I closed my eyes. I really didn't know, but I said, "Sometimes, maybe."

"I see," she said. "Nick, love is not easy. You'll have all sorts of people telling you opinions on love, especially when you're young. Some will be jealous, and jealous people want to take away your happiness. Others don't understand. They haven't felt the way you do and therefore they can't relate to you. And those are the things everyone will have to experience. You are even more special.

You have to cope with ignorant people who will judge you for even more reasons."

I shuffled in my chair. "How do I cope, mom?"

"Say your fears out loud. Let someone else help. When you say them out loud and talk about them with someone else who is strong, you'll feel better." She paused for a moment and studied me a little more closely. Then she ran her hand through my hair and said, "That means you should call Derek and tell him what's bothering you. Don't let anyone else ruin your happiness. Fear is poison to love. Don't let it poison yours. Okay?"

"Okay."

"And get your homework done, mister."

"I will."

I looked in the mirror and let Mom's words replay in my head.

Fear poisons love.

*****

"Hey," Derek answered when I called.

"Hi. Sorry I hadn't texted or talked much at all recently. I'm swamped. Homework. Practice. You know how it is."

"Yeah, it's okay. How are you?"

"I miss you."

"I miss you, too."

"I need to see you. In person. We haven't gone out since that night at Steak N Shake. That was almost two weeks ago."

"I know."

"You free tomorrow night?"

"After practice, yeah. Practices have been long though. My coach is preparing my team to play you guys again."

"Same here."

"Where do you want to meet?"

"I'll come to your place. Okay?"

"Cool. See you tomorrow."

*****

It was the longest day of school ever followed by the longest practice ever, and our teachers were not taking it easy on us with homework. I didn't know how I'd do all this damn reading and math shit and even have time to sleep, but I really wanted to see Derek.

I drove over to his house, and his mom answered the door. "Hi, Nick."

"Hi, Ms. Burka. How are you?" I didn't know if she had changed her last name or not. I hadn't asked and I had only met her briefly a couple of times when picking Derek up. She wasn't the most talkative.

"I'm alive. That's something. Come on in. Derek's in his room."

She had hardly any enthusiasm in her voice. Looking around, I saw the kitchen was a mess and the living room was dark, like there was no life in it at all.

"Thanks," I told her and went to Derek. He had a pretty sweet room. Posters of Michael Jordan hung on the wall, and movies filled up the many slots on a large DVD tower.

"Hey," he closed the door and kissed me. "I'm glad you came over."

"Me, too." I sat on his bed and thought that this could be dangerous. I wanted to be more than a bag of hormones, but when he kissed me, I could smell his delicious cologne and I already felt myself getting excited.

"So? What's up? I know we've both been swamped but if I'm being real, I've been a little worried these past couple weeks."

"Me too," I said again. "I just want to be honest with you. That's why I wanted to talk in person."

"Oh." He bit his lower lip. "Are you okay? Are we okay?"

"Yeah, totally. I love you. I really do," I said and kissed him.

"If you have to say 'really' that's not always a good sign."

"I know, but I don't mean it like that. Really." I smiled.

"Okay. So what's up?"

"I had a moment. That's all. A bad moment. Those assholes from Burlington freaked me out. I hate that it freaked me out, but it did." I looked down at my lap.

He didn't say anything. He just reached out and held my hand.

"Do you ever . . ." I continued, trying to think of the right words to explain how I felt, "Do you ever feel so . . . like happy, like I do with you, like I do with my bros, and then . . . it's like so easy for others to take that away. Do you know what I mean?" I looked up. His eyes were warm and understanding.

He nodded. "I read a lot of articles and stories people had written about being gay and coming out. One of the most common themes was that you had to find 'your people.' They'll help you be comfortable and happy. But like you said, I think there will always be 'other people.' The ones who make you want to hide, turn invisible. Or go back to a time when you didn't have to deal with them."

"Yeah, that's what I mean, that's it exactly." I paused for a moment and then added, "It's not fair, you know?"

"I know."

"No, I mean it's not fair that you're so damn hot and so damn smart. That's not fair." I smiled.

He kissed me and moved down on his bed. "Can you stay for a while?"

"Yeah," I said.

"Good." He turned on some music and locked his bedroom door.

I got hard just knowing we were going to fool around. I was very happy I came over. I would most definitely have to come more often.

*****

It was the weekend before the big game; the Tornados and the Wasps would be playing for the regional championship title tomorrow. Today, though, was something special. For me anyway. It was February 19, my birthday. I woke up and got ready for school. Looking in the mirror, I saw my now seventeen-year-old self looking back. I felt like I had aged a lot these last several months, in a good way, thanks to Derek. I imagined that there were people twice my age who hadn't experienced what I had and some perhaps who never will.

I walked downstairs and was greeted by a loud "happy birthday!" from my family. Jen, Mom, and Dad gathered around the kitchen table and had been making breakfast all morning for me.

"Dad let me make the pancakes!" Jen said.

"Remind me to skip those," I joked.

"The only thing I don't let anyone else cook is the bacon," Dad said. "It's far too valuable."

"Oh, the big seventeen! Where did all the years go? Do you remember what seventeen was like, George?" Mom asked.

"I don't remember what yesterday was like." Dad laughed. "I suspect my days weren't quite as eventful as Nick's."

"Seventeen and already in love!" Mom shook her head. "Some days I think we need to put a leash on you."

"Or at least stock up on condoms." Dad grinned.

"George! Jen is sitting right here."

"She probably knows more than all of us combined."

"Dad! Don't be weird," Jen said.

"Then I wouldn't be me."

I had an amazing breakfast and quite a few laughs, a great way to start the day.

"You'll get your present tonight," Mom said. "What time will you be home from practice?"

"Hopefully early. Coach should take it easy on us since the big game is tomorrow."

"We can't wait to see it!" Mom said. "No matter what, we have plenty to celebrate."

"I'm cheering for Derek," Jen told me matter-of-factly.

"Trader," I said.

"I think he needs someone one his side. Mom and Dad can cheer for you. I'll cheer for him."

"And we will be happy and celebrate no matter who wins," Dad said.

"Okay, you two, time to get going. See you after school," Mom told Jen and me.

*****

Thankfully, coach did take it pretty easy on us. We played a short scrimmage game and then he played a game of horse with us, one at a time while we all cheered for our teammates and taunted the coach. It was a practice of laughter and jokes, exactly what we needed before tomorrow's game. At the end of practice, he gathered us around.

"This season has been full of firsts for me. I've had players face off against friends and cousins on other teams, but never one quite as close like this. Still, I'm starting you, Nick, and the regulars.

Tomorrow is about a game, and when we're on the court, remember your team comes first. Got it?" He looked right at me.

"Yes, sir. We will win tomorrow. I know it."

"That's the attitude I want. Oh, and someone told me that we have a special birthday today. Seventeen, is it, Nick?" I nodded and he said, "As a birthday present, I want seventeen laps around the gym, then you all shower, get home and take it easy."

The team moaned and coach laughed. "And no big parties tonight, right?"

"No parties, sir," I said.

"Good. Happy birthday. See you all tomorrow. Stay focused!"

*****

I showered and got dressed, and the guys took off without saying anything to me. I thought that was pretty strange. Usually, they stick around and mess around for a bit. They had said happy birthday to me earlier, but why were they avoiding me now?

When I got home and walked through the door, I was greeted again by a loud "happy birthday!" Now I knew why they had left early. Mom and dad gathered all of my friends here. Asantà, Toby, Zack, Jared, and Darcie were there and of course my parents and Jen.

"We wanted to try and surprise you!" Jen said. "Derek is coming too. He'll be here as soon as he can."

"Aww, thanks, guys."

"I made them park down the road a ways so you wouldn't see their cars. And I've made an Italian feast," Mom said. "Lots of good carbs for you guys' big day tomorrow. So eat up!"

"Happy birthday," Asantà said. "We pitched in and got this for you. Here, man."

I unwrapped a small box to find the newest season of *Game of Thrones* on Blu-Ray. "Awesome! Thank you, guys."

"We just expect to watch it all together," Zack said.

"Definitely! Maybe we can start it Sunday after we're champs!"

"Hell yeah," Jared said. Mom gave him a look. "I mean, heck yeah!" Mom smiled with approval.

The doorbell rang, and Jen ran for the door. "Derek!" she hugged him.

"This is dangerous territory tonight." He smiled at all of us Wasps eating together.

"Tonight we're friends. Tomorrow be prepared to lose." Asantà laughed.

"I'm cheering on your side!" Jen told Derek.

"What? No way, you brat!" Jared said. He chased her around the living room. She screamed and laughed as he picked her up and spun her around. "I will make you so dizzy you won't know who you're cheering for!"

"Derek, help!" Jen cried.

"Sorry, Jen. I better stay out of this one." He turned to me then and said, "Happy birthday!" He kissed me on the lips, and again I was reminded of how nice it was to have "your people." None of my friends or family made any jokes, and they didn't look uncomfortable in the slightest. He handed me a card.

"Thanks! Can I open it now?"

"Yeah, of course."

"I just wanted to make sure it was appropriate," I grinned. I have to admit mom looked a little uncomfortable at that comment.

"It is. I promise. I saved the whips and chains for later."

It was a sweet card with a simple hand-written message. *Happy 17ᵗʰ. Love, Derek.* Inside the card was two tickets. I looked at them closely. "Oh, this is awesome. You are awesome," I said and kissed him again.

"What is it?" Dad asked.

"Two tickets to Six Flags in Chicago!"

"The park doesn't open for a couple more months, but I pre-ordered them. To continue our amusement park adventures."

"It's the best. Thank you."

"Okay, boys, sit down and get some dinner," Mom said. "Now, all of you tell me, who is going to win tomorrow?"

You can imagine Asantà didn't shut up about how we would be the winners, and Toby, Zack, and Jared chimed in with a few extra reasons. While they were listing the great decree as to why the Wasps were the best, I reached over to Derek and held his hand.

"I don't care who wins," I whispered.

"I'm excited because all this basketball stuff will be over soon. Then I can see you more often."

"Let's celebrate that, no matter who wins, tomorrow night."

"Deal."

I squeezed his hand and smiled even bigger, thinking of all of the fun ways we could celebrate. Just the two of us.

Chapter Nineteen

Good luck tonight! You'll need it. I texted Derek in the morning. It had been a few hours now, and I hadn't received a reply.

I stared at my phone, and Dad told me, "Thank God we didn't have texting when I was young. We had to leave messages at home and wait hours or even days for a reply. This instant messaging creates instant gratification, and no one has an ounce of patience anymore."

"Uh huh," I mumbled, ignoring him.

"Did you enjoy your party, Nick?" Mom asked.

"Yeah, mom, it was awesome. Thanks again."

"Good. It was nice to have all of your friends here."

Jen came out wearing all grey and white. "Oh c'mon." I laughed. "Aren't you going a little overboard?"

"Wait till you see how mom paints my face!" Grey and white were the Tornados' colors, and Jen was going all out. "It doesn't mean I'm not rooting for you, too. I just want Derek to have some support."

"I know. Still a brat though." I smiled and checked my phone for the hundredth time. Still no message. Impatient as my Dad thought, I sent another text, *Hey. U up and ready?*

A couple more hours passed, and I had to go to school and meet up with the team. I still hadn't heard from Derek. I replayed everything in my mind from the night before. Did I do something wrong? I thought we both had a pretty great night.

Asantà saw me checking my phone and said to the team, "Phones away, guys. Minds on one thing and one thing only tonight: Victory!" He looked directly at me, and I frowned but put the phone away. Worrying wasn't going to change anything right now, except for my focus on the game.

We got dressed and pumped ourselves up, cranking music in the locker room. When we warmed up, I glanced at the other side of the court. The Tornados were shooting around, but I didn't see Derek. This was getting very strange.

The gym was filling up with guests. It was our biggest crowd ever. Both sides of the gym were packed, and all of the band and cheerleaders were making plenty of noise to fire up the crowd.

The buzzer went off, and it was time for starting lineups. The Tornados were introduced first, and I smiled, remembering the torture and joy of hearing Derek's name announced months ago. It's funny: I had always thought you could find anything online, but thinking back I remembered that I could never find him. In one random day, everything in my life had changed. I laughed out loud, and Asantà gave me a weird look. I waved and mumbled "nothing." I wanted to see Derek run out and hear his name again. The roars from the crowd, the music from the band, the adrenaline in my veins, and the butterflies in my stomach: there was a lot happening right now, but all I wanted was to scream a bit myself when Derek entered the court.

But that was the problem.

He didn't.

He wasn't announced in the starting lineup. I didn't see him sitting on the bench. My mind was completely distracted. I didn't hear my own name when our starting lineup was called, and coach shoved me to move out on the court. When the game began, Jared—tall and powerful as ever—tipped the ball right in my hands, I froze. I looked all around. No Derek. One of the Tornado guards approached me and I couldn't help but ask, "Where's Derek?"

"No one knows, man. He didn't show up. He didn't call anyone and he didn't show up."

I called a time out.

"What in the hell are you doing?" Coach was furious. "We need those timeouts!"

"I can't play. I'm sorry. I . . . I have to go."

"What?"

"I have to go!"

I ran up to the stands where my parents were sitting. Bewildered, coach put in another player and the game continued without me. Zack, Toby, Jared, and Asantà looked confused and worried. Coach said to them, "I don't know what his problem is, but you guys have to keep your heads in the game. This is the biggest game of your lives right now! Let's play ball!"

"Mom. Dad." I was breathing hard from running of the bleachers, but more so because I felt absolutely sick. "Something is wrong."

"What, honey, what?" Mom asked.

"Derek isn't here. He didn't show up. He hasn't returned my texts all day. Something must be wrong. Please. I have to go look for him."

"We will help you. Let us get your sister." Dad motioned for Jen, who was watching us like a soap opera, to come over. We ran and met her outside the gym entrance.

"I'm trying to call him," I said. His cell phone rang and rang but no answer. "Derek- where are you? Please call me back. Everyone is worried. The game has started and no one knows where you are." I hung up. I searched the crowd before we left. "I'm looking for his mom," I told my family. I scanned carefully, my senses heightened, but I didn't see her. I did, however, see Eliana, and she was already coming my way.

"Nick!" she yelled. "Where's Derek?"

"I don't know! Have you heard from him at all today?"

"No," she said.

"He didn't show up, and I can't reach him by phone. Do you know his mom's number?"

"Yes, I have it in my phone. I'll call her."

We huddled around Eliana and she called Derek's mom. Every second felt like eternity, and I wanted to jump and punch something. Standing still was so hard.

"Hello? Hello! This is Eliana. Is Derek there?"

His mom answered. Thank God. We'd get some answers. I stood there listening, wanting to grab Eliana's phone and talk directly to his mom.

"What do you mean? He didn't come home last night?"

My heart sank.

"Yes, yes, I know you must be mad at him, but he's not with us either. Nick is here. The game has started. Why aren't you here?"

I felt like I was covered in chicken pox. If I couldn't grab the phone from her hands, I would scratch and tear at myself.

"No, listen to me, no one has seen him. He's not here with us. He's missing."

She listened to his mom for another moment.

"That's the best thing to do, I think. You do that. Now. And we're coming over. We're helping."

Eliana hung up. "Derek never came home last night. His mom thought she stayed with you, and she was furious that he didn't call to check in. She said she had been trying to reach him but he didn't answer her calls either. She didn't come to the game because she was mad. But he didn't stay with you, right?"

"No," I panted. "He left, when . . . around ten?" I looked at my parents who nodded.

"She's calling the police. I told her we'd be right over to help."

"Oh my God, what could have happened?" Jen cried.

"I don't know. But if he didn't get home, I want to retrace his steps. Let's split up. Mom and Jen, how about you ride with Eliana and go to Derek's house and start there with his mom? Dad, you come with me. We'll drive back to our house and retrace Derek's steps. Okay?"

"That's a good plan," Dad said. "Let's go. Call me when you get there," he said to my Mom.

"I love you, Nick. It will be okay." She kissed my cheek.

"C'mon, Dad." I didn't even look in the gym on our way out. Biggest game of our lives or not, it really didn't mean anything at all.

*****

"Oh my God. Dad! Look! How did we not see that today?" Derek's car was parked down the road from our house.

"Jesus!" he said. "I don't know. Your friends all parked down the street so you wouldn't see their cars and ruin the surprise for your party. Derek was the last to arrive. He would have parked the furthest away."

We pulled over, and I ran to Derek's car. It was locked, and he wasn't inside it. I looked in the window, but I didn't see anything weird.

"Something happened to him right as he was leaving last night. It had to have happened between our house and here!"

Dad nodded and his eyes told me that I must be right. "I'll call your mother. She'll need to tell Derek's mom. And then I'll call the police. They'll need to start here."

Dad made his calls and I was losing my mind. My walk morphed into a standing crawl, and I studied every piece of sidewalk, road, and grass from Derek's car to my house. Only one thing caught my eye. Close to our house, near the driveway, was a random roll of toilet paper. I picked it up and studied it. It was a full roll but thin, the one ply kind like they have at our cheap ass school.

I sat down on the driveway, holding the roll of toilet paper. Dad was still on the phone, and I hoped the police would get here soon. Had I found something? Some kind of clue? I didn't know. I squeezed my fists and the roll of paper, and I let out a scream that had been bottled up deep down inside me.

The tears came next.

*****

"Slow down, please. We're listening, but you have to slow down," a policeman told me.

I took a deep breath and tried to focus. "Derek is my boyfriend. We had been harassed for a long time by the basketball team at Burlington. The guys were huge homophobic jerks. They did something to him. I know it!"

"What makes you say that?" The police officer studied me and wrote down some notes.

"Look here! What's a toilet paper roll doing outside the house? Doesn't it make sense? They came here to teepee the place, and Derek must have walked outside before they got started. They dropped a roll here. Then they took him. It has to be them!"

The policeman whispered something to his partner, and she jogged back to their car. "She's going to make contact with the Burlington police right now. We'll have someone check out the homes of the players. Do you know their names?"

"Their first names, yes, but it shouldn't be hard to find since they are on the team, right?"

"Right. We'll find them. Okay, what are their names?"

I told them, and he ran off to join his partner. I sat cross-legged on the concrete driveway and put my head in my hands. Dad sat down next to me and put an arm around my shoulders.

"It's going to be okay," he said rather unconvincingly.

"Why would they take him, Dad? Why wouldn't they just have beat him up and left him here? Doesn't it mean something much worse if they took him?"

"We don't know for sure that's what happened, Nick."

"I do! Those assholes. They hated us. HATED us. They saw him alone and they took him. Dad? Would they . . ." I didn't want to say it, but I was thinking it. This was THE big thought that had slept somewhere in my subconscious since that day those assholes made fun of us in public. It was the fear that some jerk, due to jealousy, ignorance, or hatred, would want to take our happiness away.

I looked at my Dad hard and the tears rolled down my cheek. "Do you think they'd . . ."

"It's going to be okay," Dad interrupted me. "It's going to okay."

I just wasn't sure I believed him.

Chapter Twenty

Mom and Jen pulled up soon thereafter, and Eliana and Derek's mom were with them. His mom was crying, and she ran over to me.

"What happened to *my* son?" she cried.

Dad explained our conversation to the police, summarized my theory, and told her what the cops were doing. "They're starting with the boys from Burlington. They will interview them, search their houses. They're going to find your son."

"You stupid fucking kid!" She didn't look at me, but I knew it was directed at me. "What have you done to my son?"

My tears and anger were swallowed at the shock of her. "What? I didn't do anything?" I defended.

"He would have been at home if not for you. No, you two have to go flaunt your lifestyle for the world to see. And do you see what happens? Bad things happen. Bad things! Why can't you just be normal?" She wiped her nose on her sleeve.

"Excuse me," Dad said and stood up. "I know you're upset, and you have every right to be upset. But not at my son."

"God damn gays," she snarled.

"God damn gays?" It was my mother who jumped in this time. "You weren't even at the game today! God damn gays? How about god damn ignorant parents who don't support their children? YOU are the tragedy here! It's people like YOU who hurt your son, and people like YOU who are the reason bad things happen!"

"How dare you, you bitch!" she snapped back. "How dare you accuse of me of . . ."

"STOP!" Jen cried. "Stop, please." She started sobbing. My mom embraced her and shook her head at Derek's mom.

"It's going to be okay, sweetheart," Mom tried to calm Jen and herself. "It's going to be okay."

"It better be okay or I will . . ." Derek's mom started to say, but Dad interrupted her.

"You will sit down and calm down or I will call the police on you," he stated. "Now, shut up and worry about what's most important right now. Finding Derek and praying that he is unharmed."

She cried then, hands on her face, tears pouring down. Eliana looked like she might comfort her for a moment, but instead she sat down next to me on the driveway.

"I will kill those bastards. If they hurt one hair, I will kill every one of them," Eliana said. I put my arm around her and we waited.

And we waited.

*****

The police returned within the hour. "Which one of you is Derek's mom?" one asked.

"I am," Ms. Burka stated with authority and walked away from us. "You talk to me."

The police officer still spoke loud enough for us to hear. "Okay. Well, ma'am, we've made contact with the Burlington basketball team. They are being questioned right now. We don't have any information other than that to give you, but we've gotten search warrants and are checking for whereabouts and alibis of each of the boys around the time your son left the party last night. We have all the boys Nick described. If they did something, we'll know very soon."

"Very soon isn't good enough!" she shouted.

"I promise we are working as efficiently and quickly as possible. Will you be staying here for now?"

His mom looked back at us. "It's cold out. We should go inside," Dad suggested. "I'll make some coffee, and you are welcome to stay as long as needed."

"I guess I'll be here," she mumbled. "What's that dog?" She pointed at a cop who was walking on a dog on a leash.

"Those are our police dogs, ma'am. We're also going to search the neighborhood and all the yards."

"Oh, God!" she cried. "You think he could be dead lying in a ditch somewhere?"

"Ma'am, we're just being as thorough as possible to find your son. I suggest you take Mr. Revel up on his invitation, go inside, have some coffee, and warm up. We'll be in constant contact with you throughout the night."

My phone rang then, and I jumped, praying I'd see Derek's name on the caller ID. But no, it was Asantà.

"Can you guys come over?" I answered. No time for hello.

"What's going on?"

"Derek's missing. He never made it home last night. His car is still parked here. We never noticed. I think those bastards from Burlington did something."

"Shit. We'll be over in a second. Oh, shit, sorry, Nick. Damn. On our way." He hung up.

I didn't even know who won the game, I thought hazily.

I went inside with my family, Derek's mom, and Eliana. "The guys are coming over," I said. Then I sat down on a chair in the living room and took turns staring at my phone and staring at the wall.

*****

Asantà, Zack, Toby, and Jared arrived. Darcie was with them too, and they ran into the living room. "Tell us everything," Zack said.

I told them what I knew, what I thought, and what the police were doing. "Oh, Nick, I'm so sorry," Darcie said and hugged me.

Ms. Burka was pacing the living room and gave my friends all dirty looks. A few minutes later, the police arrived.

"We have some updates." Everyone sat still and hung on every word. "First, we didn't find anything in the neighborhood with the dogs. That's good. That's always a case of no news is good news." Derek's mom let out a sob, and the policeman continued. "We've also interviewed the Burlington boys and searched their homes. There's no sign of foul play at any of their houses, and their story holds up. Each has confirmed the same story. It seems, Nick, that you're at least half right about what happened last night." I shuffled in my seat, and I felt the burn of Ms. Burka's eyes accusing me still. "They did come to throw toilet paper at your house. They said they were going to do it as a joke before your big game. They parked down the street, the opposite direction where Derek's car is parked. They ran up to the house, and then they spotted him. They claim he was leaning on the driver's side of a car that had parked behind his. Then Derek got in the car." It was as if the air had been sucked out of the room. *He got in to a car?* Whose car? What did that mean?

"They didn't see any force or foul play," the officer continued. "They said he seemed to willingly get in the passenger side of the car. The car turned around, and the boys ran and hid, and that's probably when they dropped one of the rolls of toilet paper. When the car drove by, they were too freaked out to continue with their tee-pee plans, and they left."

"Bullshit!" Ms. Burka said. "They were here! They had to have done something."

"Each has backed up the story individually. It seems solid." The cop stood straight and held contact with Ms. Burka.

"Are you keeping them in custody?" Dad asked.

"We have nothing to charge them with at this time. They've been sent home with their parents with specific instructions not to leave their homes in case we do need further questioning."

Mom stood up. "Did they see what kind of car it was? Or the person in the car he left with then?"

"Each confirmed that they saw a maroon colored car, but they didn't catch the make or model, the license plate, whether it had two or four doors, or even the gender of the driver."

"What are you doing next?" Ms. Burka asked.

"We've issued an Amber alter and for anyone to call in a maroon car with a teenage passenger. We're continuing to search, ma'am. In the meantime, stay here. Amber alerts have been very effective. We have the entire state looking for Derek now."

The cops talked to Ms. Burka privately then, and I wondered what else they were telling her. The guys and Darcie leaned in close to me and Eliana. "This is bullshit," Jared said. "I don't trust those Burlington assholes. I say we find them and talk to them."

"Yeah," Asantà agreed. "We should do our own investigation."

"Let's do it," I said. "I can't sit here and do nothing and wait for answers. Something's not right. Maybe we can get info out of them that they didn't tell the police."

"Will your parents let you go?" Darcie asked.

"I don't know, but I'm going. How about you guys say you're running out to get some food. I'll sneak out the back and meet you."

"Me too," Eliana said. "I'm going with you."

"Okay," I said. "Let's find him."

The boys and Darcie stood up and Asantà announced, "We're gonna grab some fast food. Anyone want anything?" My parents shook their heads. No one appeared to be in the mood to eat.

"Okay. Be back soon," Asantà said.

"I need some water. Eliana, want some?"

"Yeah, I'll come with you," she said to me.

We went to the kitchen, and I grabbed a pen and a sheet of paper from one of the junk drawers.

"Looking for Derek," I wrote. "Can't sit here. Love you. I'll have my phone on me. – Nick." Then Eliana and I crept out the backdoor and ran into the front of the house.

"How do we split up? How do we find out where they live?" I asked.

"Nick, you and Eliana and Darcie come with me." Like the captain he was, Asantà was a natural at taking charge. "Guys you drive separately. I have a cousin at Burlington. I'll ask him to look up addresses in the school directory or something. We'll take Michael's house first. You take Frederick's. We'll go from there. Cool?"

"Perfect," I said. "Let's move. I've wasted too much time sitting here."

"We'll find him, Nick," Darcie said.

"I hope you're right."

Like a scene from *The Fast and the Furious*, we got in the cars and flew down the street.

*****

"Got it!" Asantà said. "I'll program Michael's address in my phone and let Siri guide us there."

"That's what I wanted to hear," said Eliana behind the wheel.

"What do you think happened?" Darcie asked.

"I really don't want to even think about the possibilities. I just want to find him," I answered.

"Agreed," Eliana spoke up. "Find him and hope we don't need to plan revenge."

"This is unreal," added Asantà. "What's wrong with people?"

"We don't know if it's a gay thing or any kind of thing at the moment," Eliana replied. "Right now, focus on finding him. That's all that matters."

"Can we go any faster?" I asked.

"Fuck, yeah," Eliana said. "We get pulled over, I'll tell the damn cops to keep up." She hunched over the wheel, her broad shoulders as wide as the seat, and with forceful determination, sped forward.

My knee bobbed up and down. Asantà put his hand on my leg. "Dude, he's gonna be okay." Darcie turned around from the front passenger seat and smiled weakly. We drove in silence, listening only to the hum of the engine for a good twenty minutes outside of town.

"Your destination is on the right," Siri announced from Asantà's phone, and we pulled in front of a large farm house, white and two stories high.

"Is anyone else thinking of *Texas Chainsaw Massacre* right about now?" Eliana asked.

"We're in the middle of nowhere," Darcie shook her head. "I don't know if this is safe."

"If the person behind that door isn't a good guy, then it's not safe at all. Let's hope he's not as bad as we think." Asantà opened the rear door and got out first. The rest of us followed, cautiously. I hadn't felt this scared in a long time, maybe never. The only fear I had experienced was mental. Fear about who I was; fear about what others would think or may have said. This was the first time I felt endangered physically. My stomach gurgled, even though I had nothing to eat. Standing there, trying to figure out what to do next, I jumped a mile when my cell phone went off.

"Oh, shit. It's my mother. Is she just now seeing my note?"

"She's a little distracted. Especially with the bat shit crazy mom Derek has to put up with," said Eliana.

"Mom, hey," I answered. "I can't talk now."

"Where *the hell* are you?"

"I have to call you back. I'm sorry. Please don't be mad. I'm okay. We just had to do something."

"Nick, you tell me right now—" and then I hung up on her. For the first time ever. Oh, boy. I just hoped everything turned out to be good enough for her to still be mad about that later.

Silencing my phone, I said, "You all ready?"

"Let's go," Asantà said. We walked up the front door, like a small platoon marching to battle. I had no idea what we would say or do when we got there. The cops said that the guys they interviewed weren't supposed to go anywhere. Michael should be home. Michael, one of the bastards who mocked Derek and me. If he hurt him, I'd kill him. I really would.

Thump, thump, thump. Asantà knocked. "Just a minute," an annoyed male voice said from inside. "Who the hell are you?" an older man asked, opening the door. It must have been Michael's father.

"We need to talk to Michael," Asantà stated.

"And again, in case you're deaf, who the hell are you?"

"We're friends. Friends looking for Derek," Darcie jumped in.

"That faggot? My son is no friend of a faggot."

"I see where we gets his pleasant demeanor from," Eliana told him. "Father a douche, son a douche."

"Girl, you know you're standing in front of my house. I'll call my cops and get the shotgun. But not in that order."

"I'll call the cops now and be happy to tell them the way you've just talked about a missing person," I said. "You send Michael out now, or I call the cops." I took out my cell phone and pretended to dial.

He looked at me with anger and annoyance in his eyes, wearing nothing but a stained white t-shirt and what actually appeared to be a woman's sweatpants. He snorted through his nose, but caved in. "Fine. Michael! Get down here!"

"What is it now?" Michael asked, coming from an upstairs bedroom. His feet hit the ground hard and he slumped like someone too big for his house. Then he saw us. "What the fuck are you doing here?"

"We need to talk," I said and tried to understand the evil in his eyes. "Please," I added, trying to make him feel more comfortable. "We just need answers."

"I don't have any." He was annoyed but he turned to his father and said, "It's okay, dad. I'll talk to them."

"Keep it quick. It's late." His dad looked at us one more time, shook his head, and walked away.

"What happened? What did you see?" I demanded.

"I told the police everything," he repeated. The four of us stood tall, not going anywhere. "We were gonna tee-pee your house," he said to me. "Nothing bad. Just some damn toilet paper is all."

"Did you hurt him?" Eliana asked. He looked stunned, and she took another step closer to his face.

He held up his hands. "Hey. No. I may not like him or any fag but I wouldn't hurt him."

"The way you talk isn't very convincing," Darcie told him.

"Why is that?" he looked genuinely confused.

"Let me tell you something, man," Asantà said. "You think you could talk about me and say 'nigger' and make it not sound like you're an asshole?"

"I didn't call you that! What are you talking about?"

"You say fag as easily as you say any word. It's as bad a nigger or anything else you can think of. It's rooted in hate. Period. That's why we don't believe you," Asantà stated.

Michael leaned back against the shut front door. "I didn't mean it like that."

"But hate is the only thing that word means," I said.

He was silent for a minute and studied me. "I'm . . . . I'm . . . I'll tell you what I know, okay?"

"That's all we want," I said.

"Okay. We're getting ready to throw the toilet paper. Your man Derek walks out of your house. We hide and watch where he goes. Then a car pulls up. It was maroon. The cops pressed for a lot of other details, but we weren't paying attention. We were watching your house to see if anyone else was coming out. Derek and whoever was in the car talked for a while. Then he got in and drove off with him."

"It was a man then in the car? The police weren't sure," Eliana said.

"No, I don't know, I was just being general."

"Think hard. Please. Something else. Something you may not have remembered to tell the police," I said.

"I don't know what. It wasn't violent. No one yelled or anything. I didn't see a gun or a weapon or something weird. We didn't even think he had been taken. We had no idea till the cops said he had been missing since last night."

"So it was someone he knew?" Darcie asked.

"It had to be someone he knew. It was very casual," Michael answered.

"There's got to be something. Something to help us figure out what happened," Asantà said.

"Give me your number. Like I told the cops, if I can think of anything, I'll call, okay?"

The four of us looked at one another, trying to think. Do we give up? Is this a dead end? Did we come all this way for nothing? I really thought Michael might try to hurt us, to fight us, to do whatever he may or may not have done to Derek. My fears didn't come true. He wasn't the bad ass monster I thought. Especially when he was alone, looking at four people, concerned for the life of a friend.

"Okay," I said. "Thanks anyway."

"Hey Nick," he said. "I'm . . . I'm sorry. Really."

"Thanks."

We got back in the car and tried to figure out where to go next.

My phone had five missed calls and twice as many texts from my parents. I read through the texts and listened to the voice mails. Unfortunately, all were of the angry "get your ass home" nature and had no other good news. I texted them both back, 'I'm okay. We're out looking for Derek. Can't sit still and can't be on the phone or I'm not looking as hard as I can be. I know you'll understand. Love you.'

"So where to?" Darcie asked.

"I don't know," I said. "Did you believe Michael?"

"It might sound crazy, but yeah, I did," she said. "You guys?" They all nodded.

"I expected a fist fight or something. I don't know what," I said.

"If he's telling the truth," Asantà started, "then Derek got in a car with someone he knew. Who else would he know? Who else would he get in a car with late at night? Who would he trust like that?"

"No clue," I said and then I started laughing. Maybe it was a weird reaction to all the stress, but I added, "I feel good for the first time today. If it's someone he knows, then he's probably fine, right?"

"Then why hasn't he called anyone?" Eliana said, making my smile disappear. "Something's still wrong."

"Let's check in with the other guys," Asantà said. "I'll call Jared." He dialed the number and waited for a moment. "Hey. I'm puttin' ya on speaker, okay? What did you find out?"

"We talked to Frederick. When we got there, he was actually Skyping with Jason. Frederick let us in his room, and we got to talk to Frederick in person and Jason over the computer. They were pretty shocked to see us, but they weren't the assholes we expected."

"I think the cops messed with them," Zack shouted into the phone.

"Yeah," Jared said. "Something messed with them."

"So what did they tell you?" I asked.

"The same shit they told the cops. Nothing changed in their story, not a word, man."

"Damn."

"What did you find out from Michael?" Toby yelled into the phone.

"The same. The exact same."

"One thing I didn't expect though. Frederick kinda apologized. Jason nodded and kept his mouth shut. For some guys, not being an ass is about as close to understanding as it comes," Jared explained.

"Same with Michael. So who could it be? Who could have been driving that car he got into then?" Darcie wondered.

"Maybe it's someone he used to know. Someone he used to trust," Eliana suggested. "You know, I may have an idea. It would probably be scarier than any of the guys we talked to tonight, but it's worth a shot."

"Who?" I swallowed hard and my throat hurt.

"Just trust me. Guys," she said to everyone. "Can you meet at the Steak N Shake we hang at?"

"Yeah, sure," Jared said. "Where are we going from there?"

"Meet there first. And buckle up. We've got some miles to cover," she said, and we drove off again into the night.

Chapter Twenty-One

We met up with the other guys at our planned location, and they followed in their car behind us.

"I forgot all about his dad." I was surprised when Eliana suggested we check out Derek's dad's house. She knew where he had moved after the divorce. Eliana and Derek, evidently, had driven out there before just to see where he lived. I remembered Derek telling me about his coming out story. His dad completely rejected him, and his mother wasn't a whole lot better, but the tension between the parents led to a divorce. That's at least something for Ms. Burka. She didn't abandon her kid, and she put Derek first.

"How can a father do a dick move like that to his own kid?" Asantà asked as I explained the story Derek had told me. "If I ever have kids and ever get to see them grow up and love another person, I want to be there to see that."

"He lived inside his own world. He'd come home from work and get right on the computer and look up all his right-wing nut job theories. He had a calendar of hot female conservatives," Eliana described. "That should tell you something."

"My family is conservative though," Darcie said. "I don't get it."

"There's conservative when it comes to like spending money and shit," Eliana tried to explain. "And then there's conservative like the Earth is only a few thousand years old, the devil planted dinosaur bones to fool us, and all gays are evil."

"I hate politics," I said. "No matter what you think, someone hates you for it."

"But you also can't sit back and not be involved," Eliana stated. "How do you think some of these creeps get to power? Because assholes like Derek's dad votes for them."

"True," Asantà stated. "True. So we need a plan when we get to his dad's place."

"Let me talk to him," Eliana said. "He knows me. I'll tell him his son is missing and see how he reacts. The rest of you should probably stay in the car."

I nodded, but I wasn't completely satisfied. I wanted answers. I wanted to find Derek now.

We finally pulled up in front of Mr. Burka's house. There was no car in the driveway. It was a small brick home with one large window in the front. There was at least one light on, but no sign of movement.

"Okay, wait here. For now. I'll motion if I need you," Eliana told us and got out of the car. Toby, Jared, and Zack pulled up behind us, and Eliana walked over and told them the plan.

"I don't like sitting here," I said.

"Me neither," Asantà agreed.

"She's the only one who knows him. Let's see what she can do," Darcie tried to calm us.

"What are you doing?" Asantà asked me as I started rolling down the window.

"I want to be able to hear. Don't you?"

Eliana knocked on the door, and a large man with a beard appeared. He shared Derek's raven black hair, but other than that, they didn't look very similar. This man was fat with a thin beard covering his face, wearing jeans and an Indianapolis Colts T-shirt.

"Eliana? Is that you? What are you doing here?" His voice was surprised.

"I don't know if anyone has told you, Mr. Burka, and I didn't know your phone or I would have called. Your son is missing."

He didn't respond immediately, and I wondered why his face didn't change at all. He wore a rather calm expression.

"What do you mean? What happened?"

"He disappeared last night. No one has seen him in twenty-four hours now. He even missed a big basketball game today."

"Hmmm."

"Hmmm? I thought you would be concerned."

"He probably found some queer and took off for San Francisco."

"I don't get you," she said. "Aren't you concerned at all? He's your son for God's sakes."

"The truth is, Eliana, I don't have a son. Now get off my porch." He slammed the door in her face and shut the living room curtain tight.

"We heard everything," Darcie told Eliana when she returned to the car. "Now what?"

"We're not leaving until I have a look in that garage," Eliana said. I got out of the car, and Asantà followed right behind me. He motioned to the guys in the other car to stay back.

"Careful. Maybe we should wait a minute. I'm sure he's watching," Eliana cautioned.

"Yeah, Nick. Eliana has a point. Let's pretend to drive away and then we can sneak up and take a look in the garage," Asantà suggested.

"Yeah, okay," I agreed. We got back in the car and drove down the street. Seconds felts like hours and I wanted answers now. "Has it been long enough?"

"Let's leave the car parked out of sight from his house and walk back," Eliana said.

"Just me and Nick," Asantà insisted. "Less is more. We don't want to get spotted."

"Be quick and be safe," Darcie pleaded. She leaned forward and gave him a quick a kiss.

"You know it," Asantà said and pulled away. "Let's go," he told me.

Eliana had parked a bit down the road and the other guys followed, completely out of sight from Mr. Burka's house, and Asantà and I jogged up the road to the driveway. It led behind the house where a single car garage sat. We crept past the front and got behind the home, about another twenty feet to the garage. We paused and listened but didn't hear anything. There was a back door here, and it was dark inside. I motioned for Asantà to follow me.

We approached the garage ever so slowly and looked in the windows. It was hard to see in there, too. Pitch dark outside; pitch dark inside. I took out my phone and turned on the flashlight to get a better look.

We gasped. Sitting inside the garage was a maroon colored car. Of course, a thousand thoughts flew through my head. Coincidence? It's not exactly a rare color. Or would Derek's dad somehow have found him at my house? How would that even have been possible? And if Derek is here with his father, why hasn't he let someone know?

"What now?" I asked Asantà.

"Shit, man, this is crazy. Let's get out of here before we get spotted and tell the rest of the crew." We ran back, quicker than any sprint down the court or suicide drill we ever experienced, and told the rest of the gang.

"I don't remember his dad's car at all," Eliana admitted. "But that's too much of a coincidence to let it fly."

"We should call the police," Darcie stated.

"Yes, we call the cops first," I said. "Then I'll call my parents, let them know what's up so they can tell Derek's mom. But if it is Derek's dad who took him, then we have to keep an eye on the house. If he's on to us, he may do something fast. Take off somewhere else. Or . . . or who knows what. Okay?"

"Solid," Asantà said. "Let me call the cops. You call your mom. Save some time."

"Okay."

We took out our phones, but before anything happened, we stared at each other, yelled "shit," and put our phones away.

"Anyone got service?" I asked. We were in the middle of nowhere, and everyone took out their phone to try and dial.

"Nothing, shit."

"What do we do now?" Darcie asked.

"If we can't call the cops, we have to get in that house. We have to make sure Derek is safe. Right?" Eliana said.

"Right. We only checked the garage. We can at least look around, see if there's any other sign. Keep checking our phones. Maybe we can connect to Wi-Fi at his dad's. You girls get in one car and drive off until you get a signal. I just can't leave, can't wait any longer," I said.

"Don't do anything stupid. We'll get a signal in minutes, and the cops will be on their way," Eliana said.

"We'll be right back." The girls got in their car and drove off until they could find a signal, and the starters of the Worthless High Wasps marched towards Mr. Burka's house.

*****

We crept around the front porch to the opposite side of the driveway. From the front, the house looked dark and ominous, perhaps only a perception to hypersensitive young minds, but at the moment in time, it could have the world's scariest haunted house.

Exploring the side opposite of the driveway, we looked for light through the windows. Near the back, from a small basement window, a soft light glowed and attracted our attention. "There," I pointed and spoke softly. We hit the ground and crawled on all fours, sneaking up on the window like a real-life mission from our Call of Duty games.

"Can you see anything?" Toby asked as I pressed my face against the window. I held a finger over my lips, wanting to be extra cautious this close to the house.

Then my heart leapt into my throat and I fell backwards. Mr. Burka walked below the window. Asantà gestured "what" with his hands, and I shrugged and held my finger tightly against my lips.

"Your friends are looking for you," Mr. Burka stated from below and our jaws dropped. Had we found Derek? Had Mr. Burka really taken him?

"What did you tell them?" a soft voice asked back. It was Derek! I would recognize that voice anywhere. My eyes grew twice as large and I stared at the guys.

"IT IS DEREK," I mouthed.

"Nothing. I need more time. More time to talk to you."

"You haven't told me anything!" Derek yelled back. "What do you want?"

"Shut up!" his dad snapped. "Let me think."

"Yesterday you find me at Nick's house. You say you want to talk, but all you've done is take away my cell phone and kept me in this damn house. I missed my game! Everyone is worrying for sure now! Don't you think they'll call the police?"

"Derek, I . . . I just needed time with you alone."

"We're alone! Talk to me!"

"Jesus. This isn't how I pictured telling you."

"Telling me what?" Derek asked.

"I need you here . . . I needed to tell you . . ."

Something crashed on the floor, like he kicked or threw a heavy object. I gasped, and the boys lunged forward to try and see better.

"You don't understand. I just needed a few minutes with you. But I couldn't tell you yesterday. When I saw you, all I could think about was . . . was who you became. And it made me sick. Ironically."

"What is it, Dad? If my friends are looking for me, you know they called the cops too. Spit it out already! You can't keep me like a prisoner here."

"It's cancer," his dad said.

"What?" Derek asked.

"Cancer. Bad. I was told I had maybe a month left, and that was a couple of weeks ago. I'm going to die."

Outside of the house, our eyes were wide with surprise and we held our breath, trying not to make a sound. We looked at one another but didn't know what to do. I wanted to shout for Derek, to let him know I was here, that I was ready to fight for him, but it seemed his father's intentions were more surprising than we had anticipated.

"Your mom left me, or . . . I guess I left her. And you. And I needed to talk to you. I don't have much time. I had to find you."

"How *did* you find me?"

"I've known your whereabouts every day since I left," his dad confessed. "I had one of those location apps on my phone sync to yours when we first bought you an iPhone. I've always known where you were. Could have found you any time."

"Why didn't you ever try before?"

"I don't understand you. I won't pretend to understand. But I'm dying, and I realized no one would be there with me. Not you. Not your mom. I'd die alone in a hospital with no one who knew anything about me."

"You did that to yourself," Derek said.

"I know. I know!" He paused for a moment. "There are so many things to say I don't know where to start."

"What happened to you?"

"Before I met your mother, a long time ago, at some college party," his dad started, "I got . . . really drunk. Whiskey, tequila, you name it, and I drank it."

"Why are you telling me this?"

"Because I'm disgusting, and if I don't confess these disgusting things now, I . . . who knows what may happen? Maybe I'll end up in hell."

I can think of some other reasons you'd end up in hell, I thought, still listening from the outside.

"What did you do?"

"I slept with a . . . with a man. Fuck. I never thought I'd tell anyone that."

"Are you telling me you're gay?" Derek asked.

"Fuck you! No, I'm not a fag. I was drunk and slept with a . . . did something so unnatural, so unforgiveable."

"Again, why are you telling me this?" I heard the pain in Derek's voice, and I curled my hands into fists. Fuck his father for doing this to him. It took every ounce of will power I had to not scream, break down the door, and take Derek away from this monster.

"I need you and your mother to be there with me, in the hospital. I don't want to die alone."

"What you did, Dad . . . what you're doing and what you've done, you did this to yourself. I'm sorry you're dying, but I won't be there at the hospital. Or your grave. Ever!" Derek shouted.

"You bastard!" his dad yelled and we heard a smack, a hard slap, skin against skin, and it made us jump to our feet.

"What do we do?" Asantà whispered to me.

I did the only thing I could think of, the only thing I had wanted to do since hearing Derek's voice: I slammed my fist on the window and yelled, "DEREK!"

"Who the fuck is there?" we heard his dad yell, and then we heard the most glorious music to our ears (never thought I'd say that as a teenager)! We heard sirens quickly approaching from the distance, and in seconds, police cars had surrounded the front of Mr. Burka's house.

Chapter Twenty-Two

Everything happened as quickly as, well, a tornado. Police banged on the door, a cop saw us and shouted "hands up" and "come out where we can see you." Mr. Burka came to the door, a lot of yelling ensued, which resulted in him getting cuffed pretty quickly. And then from behind, Derek walked out the door.

"Derek!" I yelled and stood up, but a police officer quickly interjected.

"Stay where you are!"

A moment later, more cars pulled up in front of Mr. Burka's house. Darcie and Eliana jogged up the driveway, and my parents were right behind them along with Ms. Burka.

"What's going on?" Derek's mom shouted.

"Nick, are you okay?" my mother yelled.

"Everyone calm down and stand back," another officer demanded. "Are you Derek Burka?" The officer faced the man of my dreams, he nodded, and she asked, "Tell us what's happened here."

"I'm his mother," Ms. Burka yelled and ran up to the front porch. "Oh, Derek," she cried and hugged him. Derek hugged her back, but softly and awkwardly. "What did you do?" she snapped at her ex-husband, now seated on the porch with his hands cuffed behind his back.

"Mom, it's okay. Let me explain."

"Please do," the officer said.

"Dad's dying," Derek said. "He met me outside of Nick's last night. Found my location through my phone. He . . . he didn't hurt me. He wanted to talk. That's all."

"Why didn't you call me? Why didn't you call someone?" his mom asked.

"He took my phone. It's a long story. He didn't want me leaving, and it took him until Nick showed up to get the courage to speak his truth. The point is this: he's real sick and he's dying. Like now." Derek looked at me then and frowned. I wanted to go to him, but felt stuck on the ground until the police granted permission.

"Sir," the police officer asked. "What do you have to say for yourself?"

"I needed to talk to him. That's all." Mr. Burka's head sank to the ground, defeated.

"So you picked him up in a maroon car? When did you get a new car?" his mom asked, as if that was what was important.

He sighed, his head hanging limply from his neck, not answering her question.

"All right, everyone. We'll need to question all of you, get your statements, and fill out some paperwork," the officer spoke again. "I suggest we do this at the station where it's warm. We'll take Mr. Burka. Kids, you follow Mr. and Mrs. Revel. Ms. Burka, why don't you ride with them, too?"

We all nodded and watched as Mr. Burka was escorted into the backseat of a police car. We stood up, and I charged at Derek, grabbing and hugging him tightly.

"I was so worried. Are you okay?" I asked.

"I've been better. You came all this way looking for me? How did you find me?"

"We're quite a team when we work together. Eliana thought we should check your dad's house."

Eliana smiled and hugged him then. "I think it's still going to be a long night," she said. "But we're all glad you're okay. You had us all very worried."

"Thanks," Derek said and looked at his mother. "Mom?"

Ms. Burka cried and shook her head. "Derek . . . I don't know what to think or say. There's so much to say. I don't know where to begin."

"It's okay, mom. We have plenty of time to talk. For now, let's get this night over with," he told her, and we walked to our vehicles, followed my parents, who followed the police to the station.

*****

"Don't you ever run off like that again!" Mom grilled me at the police station. "We were worried to death!"

"I know. I'm sorry, but you know I couldn't just sit there and wait."

"In the end," Dad jumped in, "it's good what you did." My mom snapped him a look, but he continued. "You found him. You got the police there. I mean, who knows what could have happened or how long this could have went on. You were brave. Stupid. But brave."

"Thanks, Dad," I said. I looked around the room, waiting on Derek. Naturally, they had spoken to him the longest. The police took my statement and all of our friends' statements rather quickly. They had called their parents, who all insisted they come straight home. It was just me, my parents, and Ms. Burka now. I told my parents I had to stay until I saw Derek.

Finally, he came out from one of the offices after talking to the police for a while. "They're taking my father to the hospital under custody for the time being. He's quite sick and needs hospital attention. They think . . . they think he'll probably die there, and soon."

I stood and put an arm around Derek. "I'm sorry. How . . . how do you feel?"

"I don't know how to feel," he said. "It's all so confusing."

"Yeah. What are you going to do?"

"Can I stay with you tonight?"

"Absolutely not," Ms. Burka said, jumping up from across the room. "You are coming home and staying home."

"Mom, I . . . I need to be with Nick. I need to be with someone who . . ." *Who loves me*, I thought he was going to say, but he didn't finish. Ms. Burka must have gotten the same message, though. She wiped newly formed tears from the corners of her eyes, and my parents gave each other a concerned look.

"What do you two think?" Ms. Burka asked my parents.

Dad looked at Mom, and Mom answered, "I guess that's okay. If it's okay with you."

"It doesn't appear that I have a choice," she answered. "Fine. But call me in the morning."

"Okay, I will," Derek said. He turned to my parents next. "Thank you," he said. "Thank you for waiting here. For letting Nick wait here. For everything tonight."

"Of course," Mom said and hugged him. Ms. Burka watched, and I could feel the jealousy squirt threw her veins. She turned, walked away, and went home. Derek and I sat in the back seat of my parents' car, my arm around his shoulders, his head pressed against me. Dad looked in the rear view mirror and smiled warmly at me. I smiled back, hoping it told him how amazingly appreciative I felt.

*****

"I have to go the hospital," Derek said the next morning. "And I want you to come with me. Please."

"Of course. What are you going to do?"

"I'm going to say good-bye to my father."

213

We had breakfast with my parents, and I told them what Derek wanted. Their eyes told me they were concerned about me going, but they didn't say anything. Mom and Jen and even Dad hugged us a lot that morning, and after eating and cleaning up, Derek and I drove to the hospital.

"Do you want me to wait out here?" I asked when we approached the room.

"No. You are a part of my life. I want him to see that, and I want you to hear what I say, too."

I nodded, and he kissed me gently outside of the room. Neither of us looked around to see if anyone cared or noticed.

We walked in slowly but confidently, shoulders tall, chin high. "Hi," Derek said to the man in the hospital bed. His father looked terrible. Hooked up to devices I couldn't describe, he seemed more machine than computer.

"Derek," he whispered. "You came." His voice was soft but audible.

"I came to tell you what I needed to tell you," Derek said with authority. "First, I want you to meet my boyfriend. This is Nick. Nick Revel. He's the greatest thing that's ever happened to me."

Mr. Burka looked at me but didn't speak for a moment. Silence filled the room, and Derek let it build like a cloud before a storm. Finally, his father spoke, "Son . . . I . . . they say I could die any day. Maybe today."

"Then it's even more important for you to meet the person I love."

Mr. Burka looked up again at me, but didn't say anything to me. "Derek," he started. "I don't have time for these games."

"It's not a fucking game," Derek barked. "He's the fucking love of my life."

"That doesn't mean I have to fucking love it," his dad said.

"Even like this, even though you could die today, that's how you choose to act?" Derek asked. I could see an anger in him that I had never witnessed. His face reddened, an anger fueled with sorrow and fury at everything an ignorant man couldn't understand.

"I just wanted to see you before I die," his father said. "And to confess my . . . sins."

"Well, here I am, but I haven't heard you confess any sin. How do you think you'll be judged for turning your back on your own son?" Derek held his hands up and sighed. "Anyway, I want to tell you some other things, too. You know what I think? I think the things we hate on the outside are the things we hate on our inside. You told me you slept with a man. You had a desire. You acted on that desire. But it scared you, terrified you, and what do you do? You decide to hide it and to hate it and to hate anyone and everyone that accepts what you hate or acts in the ways you hate. That's what I think."

"I told you I'm not—" His dad coughed.

"I don't care what you are," Derek said. "And that's the point. I don't give a damn either way. You've led a life that makes me not give a damn about you. You want me here on your death bed to say good-bye? How about trying to be in my life? How about looking Nick in the eye and saying 'nice to meet you' and accepting that I love him and he loves me and it's not disgusting at all but actually really fucking beautiful? How about that!?"

Mr. Burka pressed the call button while Derek was talking, and a nurse entered the room. "What can I do for you?" the nurse asked just as Derek finished.

"Can you please escort these two people out of my room?"

The nurse looked at us, confused. "Isn't this your son?" he asked.

"His son and his son's boyfriend," Derek answered.

The nurse turned to Mr. Burka for a response. "I don't have a son," he said. The nurse's face whitened.

"It's okay," Derek said. "I never had a father." He grabbed my hand, and we walked out of the room. Derek never said good-bye.

Chapter Twenty-Three

We sat cuddled together in my favorite spot, snuggling closely on my bed. A week had passed since Derek visited his father in the hospital. We received news that Mr. Burka had passed away on the following day. Derek built an emotional fortress and hadn't talked much about his dad's passing or the final day he visited him. Now we were trying to get back to just being us. There was a *Will & Grace* marathon on TV, and we were binge watching and enjoying a lazy Sunday afternoon together.

"Whenever I watch this show, I always wonder why my mom was shocked when I came out," Derek joked. "We watched this together a hundred times. It was our thing back in the day. How did she not even suspect?"

"You do remind me of Jack," I said.

"Whatever!" He hit me with a pillow.

"How's she doing? Your mom?"

"I don't know. I don't know if she'll ever be 'normal,' you know? She went and saw my father before he passed, but she didn't tell me much about it."

"Still no word on services?" I sat up a bit in bed, but still close to Derek.

"Mom had him cremated, but the only family really left is us. His parents are old, no other siblings. I suppose my grandparents will want to do something, but no one's made arrangements."

"What are you going to do?" I asked.

He shrugged. "If there's a service? I suppose I'll go."

"If you feel weird talking about it, you can tell me. Or we don't have to talk about it." I nudged him with my shoulder and smiled.

"Thanks." He smiled back. "I don't know what I expected at the hospital. Or what my dad expected by taking me for that day. I kept wishing he'd say sorry or find a way to explain himself. In the end, I think he just didn't want to be alone. But I couldn't be there for him, not if he wasn't even trying to know the real me. Was I wrong?"

"No," I said and cuddled up more closely with him. "Like you said, some people walk such narrow paths that they only see what they want to see. He never made room for you. It's sad."

"It is." He sighed. "Okay, enough for now. Let's watch the show. I just want to relax and not think, you know?"

"Okay," I said. "But I have one more thing I've been wanting to ask you. Not about your dad. About a . . . a night in our future. I don't know if this is the best time, but I've been thinking about and just want us to, you know, have a happy night to plan that we can look forward to. A distraction from all of this." My heart rate doubled instantly as I spoke these words.

He sat up straighter in bed and turned to me. "Oh? So what do you want to ask?" he smiled.

"Okay, here goes. It's a little over a month away, but I figure we should prepare." I stood, wanting to do this properly. I reached out, held his hand, and pulled him up. Then I dropped to one knee. "Um, so, will you . . . . will you go to prom with me?"

Derek laughed. "Damn, boy, for a moment there . . . of course, I will go to prom with you, but only on one condition," he replied. "You have to go with me to my prom, too."

"Absolutely!"

"Then it's a yes." He pulled me back on the bed with him, curled up as close as was possible, wrapped his body around mine, and kissed me. "We'll look so hot in tuxedos! Like two gay James Bonds."

I kissed him back, rather enjoying the image of Derek in a tux, and rather enjoying the image of me taking that tuxedo off of him after the dance.

"It will be the best night ever," I said.

*****

On Monday at school, Steve, the first boy I kissed, talked to me in between classes. "I know that our pride club isn't your thing, but can you stop by after school for a bit? Please? I've been working on something I think you'll like."

I nodded, feeling a bit guilty. I had never really given that club a chance. "Sure. I'll stop by."

"Great!" I watched Steve walk away, envious in how comfortable he seemed to always be in our own skin. I had judged him, too, before. That wasn't fair. He just wanted to be himself, as much as any of us want to be us.

After school, as promised, I met Steve and his freshmen female following for their gay-straight alliance club. The club had grown in membership, which was cool to see. It was a full classroom, about a dozen underclassman and several juniors and seniors as well, a good mix of guys and girls. I didn't know if they were gay or straight, and it really shouldn't matter, should it?

"Good afternoon, everyone. As promised, I have something special to announce today. I thought Nick would be especially interested, which is why I invited you here. We have some special guests on Skype who, you'll all be surprised to know, I'm gonna let do the rest of the talking."

Everyone laughed, and Steve turned on the projector. A Skype session brightened before our eyes. It was quite the surprise and not what I had expected at all. I thought Steve might want to say a few words about what Derek experienced last week and ask for my thoughts. Instead, I saw Michael from Burlington appear on the big screen in the classroom.

"Hello, Wasps," he greeted. "My name is Michael Wells. I play basketball at Burlington. I wanted to formally introduce you to the Burlington gay-straight club. We've had a few students interested in creating such a club, but it never got started. This last week, I talked to those few who had been interested, and here we are, our first meeting. I don't really know how to run a club, so we thought you might give us some pointers and maybe we can work together."

I was completely incredulous. No way! But I smiled. I went up to the front of the classroom so I could be on the camera and Michael could see me.

"Hi, Nick," he said.

"Hi, yourself. Wow, this is a surprise."

"Yeah, I know." He shrugged a bit.

"It's cool. Good for you. Anyone else from the team helping you?"

"Just me for now. But I'm working on that. I was hoping you'd be here, Nick. What I wanted to say, on behalf of the team, even if they're not here today to say it, but they will be someday, I swear." He paused for a drink of water, and his face crinkled with nervousness. "When Derek went missing and the cops thought maybe we did something to him, when you and your friends thought we might do something, we were pissed at first. But it made me think. It made me think that the shit we've said and done had actually made you all think we were capable of . . . of *that*. And maybe you're right. That's why I'm here. Not because I understand or totally get it. But because I don't want to be an asshole. I don't want to be the kind of guy you thought I was."

"It starts with one," Steve interrupted. "We're thrilled to have you as a supporter, Michael Wells."

"Thanks." Michael looked shy yet optimistic, the look of a man stepping on a bridge for the first time. "I don't really know what else to do or say. But I'm on your side, and I'll do whatever I can to rally support here, to help myself and others like me at least try to understand. It's one thing to be mean on the basketball court. It's another to think about a missing person, you know? We actually thought for a while that something really bad might have happened to Derek."

"Me, too," I said. Every time I thought about what could have happened I had to hold back the tears. I blinked them back again and managed to say, "Thanks, Michael."

"I'd be happy to tell you all about our club here, Michael and Burlington High, and everything we do to promote understanding," Steve said.

Maybe I'll come to more of these meetings, I thought, as I watched Steve address Burlington High over Skype. When it comes to elections, my dad always said you can't complain if you don't vote. Maybe the same is true for understanding people who are gay or different in all sorts of ways. We can't complain if we don't at least speak up for ourselves.

*****

That weekend the gang all decided to meet up at our usual Steak 'n Shake location. Derek would bring Eliana, Asantà would bring Darcie, and the guys invited their New Year's Eve dates. Everyone had a partner except for Eliana, but she didn't seem to mind.

It was the first time we had all gathered since that crazy weekend, and it was a little awkward at first. Derek took it upon himself to break the ice.

"So you two official?" Derek asked Darcie and Asantà.

They both looked at me before responding, and I smiled, encouraging them that it was all good. "Yeah," Asantà said. "She's my girl now."

"It's cool. She had the best guy here, so I suppose second place is the best she can get," I joked. Darcie flicked her straw at me, shooting the tiniest bit of ice cream in my face. "Yum!" I licked it off.

"You were okay," Darcie said. "Asantà is pretty great. But I think we know who the best guy here is." She smiled and flicked some ice cream at Derek.

"Aww, don't make me blush, now." Derek laughed and I lunged over and licked the ice cream off his face.

"You two keep shoving your homosexual lifestyle in our faces. You and your agendas to . . . what exactly is a gay agenda anyway?" Eliana laughed.

"Something clueless people say," Derek said.

"I thought the gay agenda was to turn people gay," I joked.

"That's right! Cuz it's a choice after all, like being a Colts fan or a Bears fan," Derek teased.

"If the world knew how awesome you guys are, it would be the end of any gay problem ever," Jared said.

"I think that's the nicest thing you've ever said. What did they put in your milkshake? And can I have some?" I asked.

"I'm serious. You two are awesome," he repeated.

"Enough of this sappy shit. I need gossip," Eliana interrupted. "Who's doing who here? Asantà and Darcie? Any below the jeans action going on?"

"A gentleman would never tell," Asantà chuckled.

Eliana looked around. "Where's a gentleman? None at this table! Excuse me, sir," she called out to our server. "We need a gentleman over here if you can find one." He gave her an odd look and smiled politely and quickly went to talk to another table.

All of the laughter relaxed us. We found our groove. A bunch of high schoolers, ex-couples, current couples, gay and straight, black and white. But there was only one real label, the one we all preferred:

Friends.

*****

At the end of the night, I drove Derek home. "Wanna come inside?" he asked.

"Um, let me ask the boss." I pretended to look inside my jeans. "Uh, okay, I guess he's up for something." I smiled and kissed him, and we stumbled all the way from his car into his living room like that.

Ms. Burka coughed, and we stopped and turned around. "Hi, Mom," Derek said.

"Yes, hi there." She shook her head. She stood up, though, and came over to us. She wrapped her arms around Derek and hugged him. He looked about as shocked as me.

When she let him go, she looked over at me. "Nick. I've been thinking a lot since Derek's father passed. Since that whole weekend. I want to tell you something, okay?" She moved closer to me and continued, "There are a lot of bad people in this world. I've seen a ton of them. There's a lot that I don't understand and I lot more I hope to understand better every day, but I'll say this. You're not one of those bad people, and I'm happy my son is with one of the good ones." She hugged me then, harder and longer than she had hugged Derek.

I reached around with one arm to hug her back, and she said, "You use two arms when you hug me, okay?" I did as she told, gave Derek a WTF look, and he simply smiled and shrugged his shoulders.

"Now," she said, letting go, "I think you both have a curfew. One more hour, okay? And then Nick should go home and sleep in his own bed. That seems like the proper thing to do, wouldn't you agree?"

"Yes." Derek grinned.

"Good. And your bedroom door stays open for that hour, too."

We nodded, and she went back to watching TV in the living room. We ran to Derek's bedroom and poked our heads out a few minutes later to make sure she wasn't checking on us. Then we shut the bedroom door all the way.

Derek kissed me hard, pulled my shirt off over my head, and took me down to his bed.

Maybe it was seeing Derek's mom try to change. Maybe it was what Derek did to my body after the door closed. Oh, boy. So many things. I'd tell you, but I've learned that a gentleman shouldn't share everything. But I will tell you this.

That night became my new favorite night. Ever.

<u>Afterward</u>

My great friend Eric was the first to read this text and give invaluable feedback. Last fall my partner and I were in Eric's wedding. Growing up, I never thought that would be possible. Congrats to you both, Eric and Brad.

To my readers: I hope you'll never encounter a Mr. Burka. I have, and I've seen the pain it can cause. So this book also goes to the bad people in the world who would rather give up their children than accept their happiness. Fuck you, but thanks for the inspiration.

I hope you will all find your Derek.

This story found success on Tapas (type tapas.io in your web browser). So much, in fact, that they encouraged me to write a follow-up. I wasn't sure I wanted to write a sequel. I like the ending. Derek and Nick are happy. Let's leave them be, right?

But a couple things happened since 2016. We've seen attacks on LGBT rights, from transgendered in the military to even a question as to whether or not LGBT are protected under the Civil Rights Act and more.

I spent a lot of time angry at the world, and when I'm angry, I create. But I also had questions about Nick and Derek.

What went through Derek's mind during the highest highs and lowest lows? And what would happen if Nick and Derek had to separate (maybe their families moved, or they went to different colleges, or you know, LIFE got in the way)? Would they find their way back to one another?

Those questions got my fingers typing again for a new book called *Looking for Nick*. This time, we get in Derek's head, but we're also going to face a big challenge in their relationship.

I hope you're excited (and just a little nervous; it's okay to be both!) and I hope you look forward to this next installment. It's available now on Tapas. Someday I'll put that story in print, too. But right now I want you to support them and go read it there. They've been AMAZING to me and so many other creators. Thank you, Tapas. Specifically, thank you Jessica Sanchez, the former senior director of content development. We've had hundreds of e-mail exchanges, and I couldn't be happier to have found some a great platform to tell my stories. I will end by giving you the first few pages of that story here.

Thank you. Feel free to follow me on Twitter and Instagram. Search for NC Nest. Thanks.

Looking for Nick

If I had to rank order the three hardest parts of my life so far, it would go like this:

The third hardest part was the day Nick Revel let some homophobic bully shut me out of his life on the very day that I thought we both fell in love.

The second hardest part was coming out to my homophobic parents.

The hardest part, though, so far: Getting ready to say good-bye to Nick Revel.

My name is Derek Burka, and I met Nick on a summer trip to Kings Island in Cincinnati, Ohio about two years ago. We had both won trips through school fundraisers. That day on the bus and at Kings Island is one I'll never forget.

It's an important day in my life, and before I tell you what's happening today, let me tell you about that love-at-first-sight day.

I saw Nick sitting by himself on the bus, and right away I wondered if he might be "family." I had only just begun to learn about things like *gaydar*, and I suppose I hoped every cute boy was like me. But Nick had a vibe—it was the way he looked at me with those brown eyes when I asked if I could sit next to him. His eyes were lit with desire. It wasn't until he pretended to fall asleep and touched my leg that I thought for sure that he was really into me.

Have you ever had that happen? Has someone ever touched you, and you weren't sure if it was on purpose? His hand slid across my leg, and I had to swallow hard and think of the book I was reading to not get excited. Even then, I felt a stir in my shorts as something began to stiffen. Oh, God. What if he touched that and none of this was on purpose? He'd probably say some disgusting words and that would be the end, right? But I'd have to think of him all weekend on this damn trip—the guy who fell asleep next to me and accidently touched my boner.

That would be awful.

At some point, I felt Nick looking at me. I turned and smiled. He smiled back and he didn't move his hand. That made be stiffen all the more, and I wondered if he had felt that. Oh, God. Say something!

"You wanna be my partner?" *What the hell did I just say? That may not have been the best choice of words.*

"What?" Nick asked. His face told me he was as shocked as me.

"On the roller coasters. Wanna ride them with me?"

"Yeah, for sure. That would be great." Nick's hand was still on my thigh, and I still had a semi-erection. That's when Brandon—let me tell you about this fucking homophobe—asked if anyone wanted to play a card game called Bullshit.

Nick took his hand away, and I tried to not to even blink. I couldn't let him know that I knew. Could I? What if Nick really was asleep and out of it and just didn't know what he was doing?

These feelings can sure suck. Talk about roller coasters.

A dozen games and a couple hours later and we were finally at Kings Island. At first, everyone was hanging out together, and I was trying so hard to be patient. I just wanted to ride with Nick—not these other people. But I smiled like nothing in the world bothered me (that's the face I tend to wear when things really do bother me), and I waited. After a bit, I finally got to partner up with Nick. I thought of him "falling asleep" next to me on that bus, and I decided this would be my time to touch him and see how he reacts.

Just as the coaster jerked back hard to begin its long ascent, I let my hand slide over to Nick's knee. I held my breath, and not out of fear of the coaster but out of fear as to how Nick would react. He didn't flinch or say anything, and I prayed that was a good sign.

When the coaster shot down a deep descent, we both screamed and Nick grabbed my hand. He was holding my hand! I couldn't believe it. My heart was beating incredibly fast, and I felt warm everywhere. It was the best feeling in the world.

Do you get that? I know all kids probably feel great the first time someone they like holds their hand. Maybe it's during recess and you hold hands with this girl you've been crushing on. Later, all the kids tease you, but somehow that kind of teasing is okay. It's an acknowledgment, even approval. You're not just a boy anymore. You're a boy who holds hands with a girl. You might as well be holding her on the edge of the Titanic and screaming out to the world.

That's special. Don't get me wrong. But there are also a few of you like me. A few of you who've never had someone you've liked romantically reach out and hold your hand. When Nick touched my leg on the bus and when he grabbed my hand on that roller coaster—it was the best damn feeling in the world.

A lot of my friends had their first kisses and first hand-holding (and some even their first hand jobs, if I'm being honest) in middle school. That gets celebrated—IF you're straight. When you're gay, no one celebrates your first kiss or your first hand-holding and definitely not your first hand job. Even if the world seems accepting on prime time TV, it's not very fucking accepting in the playgrounds and locker rooms.

I think little kids accept without judgment, but then something happens when puberty hits. If you're a guy who is not into vagina, your teen years are gonna feel like they last forever. Maybe things get better after high school. But no matter if gay marriage is legal or if your friend down the street has two gay moms, it is damn hard to be a gay kid.

Period.

www.ingramcontent.com/pod-product-compliance
Lightning Source LLC
Chambersburg PA
CBHW021012120726
47905CB00009B/2971